BLOOD
AND BONE

FROM THE OUTER REACHES ...

Blood and Bone
by Malcolm Rose

Published by Ransom Publishing Ltd.
Unit 7, Brocklands Farm, West Meon, Hampshire GU32 1JN, UK
www.ransom.co.uk

ISBN   978 178127 673 0
First published in 2015

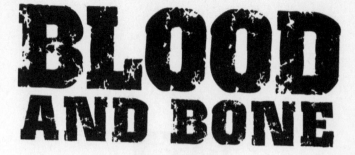

BLOOD AND BONE

MALCOLM ROSE

Ransom

By the same author

From The Outer Reaches ...

BODY HARVEST

When the body of an outer is discovered in the woods, young detective Troy Goodhart and forensic specialist Lexi Iona Four are partnered on the case. Then two more bodies are discovered, and all three corpses are found to have body parts missing. Somebody is killing with a purpose. As major Troy and outer Lexi unpick the case, they enter a complex, dark world of deception, where one false move will mean death.

LETHAL OUTBREAK

Three scientists wearing airtight protective suits are found dead in a sealed, high-security laboratory. They had been studying an unknown substance brought to Earth by the recently returned Mars probe. Was this substance responsible for their deaths? Was it an accident – or could it be murder? Young detective Troy Goodhart and forensic specialist Lexi Iona Four quickly realise that this case is about something much worse than straightforward murder.

FATAL CONNECTION

Is it a coincidence when four people die at the same time with the horrible symptoms of mercury poisoning? Especially when all four lived in different parts of the country and didn't seem to have anything in common. Is there a connection between the victims? Young detective Troy Goodhart and forensic specialist Lexi Iona Four are convinced there must be, and they set out to find the connection and arrest the killer(s). But can they stay alive long enough to solve this mysterious crime?

THE OUTER REACHES

*A world inhabited by two distinct and non-interbreeding humanoid species: **majors** (the majority) and **outers**. The two races are outwardly similar, but they have different talents, different genetics and different body chemistry.*

In this world, meet major Troy Goodhart and outer Lexi Iona Four. They make an amazing crime-fighting partnership.

SCENE 1

Thursday 15th May, Morning

Outside, the light faded rapidly, as if a thick black cloud was moving in front of the sun and a fearsome storm was on its way. There was a sudden chill and a cold wind swirled – but a change in the weather wasn't the cause.

Inside the shabby white van, the courier narrowed his eyes. If the vehicle had been more modern, it would have been programmed to drive itself, but this old model needed to be operated by a human being. Ahead of the driver, high in the sky, the moon was within seconds of completely blocking out the sun.

He knew that he shouldn't stare at the solar eclipse with unprotected eyes, but the spectacle was awesome. He knew he should concentrate on driving, but he was engrossed by the cosmic display. He was behind schedule and needed to speed his refrigerated cargo to its destination in Shepford, so he refused to let up on the accelerator. His stinging, watery eyes flicked between the road ahead and the sky above.

Just before the eclipse became total, sunshine glared from one side of the sun: a diamond smile. It dazzled him, blinding his vision. His eyes snapped shut as he approached the bend. The van left the road at speed, careered across the verge and slammed into the trunk of a tree.

For a few short minutes, the moon robbed the day of its sunlight and plunged the road into darkness. Birds ceased to sing and returned to their roosts. In the sky, only the sun's corona glimmered from behind the perfect black disc.

Realizing that the engine was fatally damaged, the driver staggered out of the van into the oddly cooled air. There was a small bloodstain on his jeans, but he didn't stop to investigate the injury. In this night-time that had struck in the middle of the morning, he had to decide what to do immediately. Given the load that he was carrying, he did not want to be found with it

– and another car could come along at any moment. The people who had hired him were not the understanding sort. He did not dare to call them, tell them what had happened and ask for help. He knew what happened to people who made mistakes.

As harsh sunlight began to return and birds celebrated the day's second dawn, the courier wiped all the surfaces he might have touched, hastily removing his fingerprints. Then he yanked off the registration plates. Making sure he wasn't leaving anything that the police could use to identify him, he made off across the field, towards the distant village.

Holding his aching neck with his right hand and the number plates in his left, he lurched and stumbled as he made his escape from the scene of the accident. He was on the run from the police and from the cruel, unforgiving gang that was paying him to make the delivery.

SCENE 2

Thursday 15th May, Afternoon

Inside the police tape that surrounded the crime scene, the large white van was an abandoned wreck. 'It's not automatic,' Detective Lexi Iona Four said. 'Someone was in control of driving it. Or *supposed* to be in control.'

'My guess is he got distracted by the eclipse,' said her partner, Troy Goodhart.

'I can understand that. It would have been a fantastic show.'

'Spooky.'

'Not spooky at all,' Lexi replied. 'Just a simple –

but spectacular – cosmic coincidence. Or do you believe in a devil that eats the sun and then spews it back up again? Or is it a sign of bad luck? Doom and disaster to follow?'

'No. It's three celestial bodies lining up. That's all. Majors used to have all sorts of superstitions to explain the sun winking out for a while. Some thought it was a sign that God was angry. But that was ages ago.'

'I wish we weren't wrapping up the last case when it happened,' Lexi said. 'I would've liked to see it. Probably got to wait three hundred years for the next one to come along.'

The uniformed officer stationed beside the crash site grinned at the idea.

Peering in through the driver's door, Lexi soon started making deductions. 'Someone's wiped this down,' she said. 'As far as I can see, there's just a few prints left and they're smeared out. No use at all. But they tell me the driver was a major.'

The fingertips of outers like Lexi were smooth and free of giveaway patterns. Only the other human race – majors, like Detective Troy Goodhart – had fingerprints.

She smiled. 'If the driver thought getting rid of fingerprints would stop me … Huh! There'll be other traces. I'll collect them later.'

As an outer, Lexi was particularly skilled in science. She was in charge of forensics. Troy was more into human nature; his strengths were in interviewing suspects and witnesses, and understanding what makes them tick.

The two young detectives continued their slow circuit of the van, making their first observations and taking photographs, before disturbing anything. Detail would come after they'd worked out what sort of crime they were investigating.

Lexi pointed at the bare bodywork where there should have been a registration plate. 'That won't stop me either. I'll trace the van through its engine number.' She squatted down and squinted at the front tyre on the left-hand side. 'Or figure out where these came from and where they've been.'

Surveying the side of the van for anything that would help her identify it – or its owner and driver – she stopped by a small blue mark. 'It's scraped against something here. There's no dent so it wasn't a big collision. More like it brushed against something bright blue. I'm taking a paint sample from that.' Then she paused.

'What's on your mind?' asked Troy.

'I've seen that shade of blue somewhere recently,' said Lexi.

Troy frowned. 'It's like my shirt – and the car we came in. And lots of other blue things.'

'I know but … ' Lexi shrugged. 'We'll see.'

Using a scalpel, Lexi scraped the sample into a small evidence bag. Then they both walked to the rear of the van.

Troy hesitated by the back doors. 'Ready to go in?'

'Yeah. According to the person who called the police, this is where it gets interesting.' She opened the double doors, let in the sunlight and at once the mood changed. She uttered a cry of disgust.

The uniformed officer looked over his shoulder at her. He was curious but stayed where he was, on guard.

Troy and Lexi stood outside the vehicle, staring into the back. Lexi took photographs, before they climbed in gingerly. The space resembled a butcher's shop. Down one side were stacks of meat, bottles of blood, jars containing eyeballs, a large stack of bones, and sealed tanks holding grey wrinkly brains in a clear liquid. Opposite, there were more carcasses, a crate with a jumble of horns, rows of small plastic boxes containing teeth, hair, whiskers and claws, and animal skins draped over racks. Some of the skins were immediately identifiable. The stripy orange, black and cream ones were obviously from tigers. Others were leathery and less distinctive.

Stooping, the detectives tiptoed down the aisle in between. Troy swallowed and whispered, 'This is grotesque.'

'Oh, it's more than that,' Lexi replied, clearly appalled and desperately angry. 'It's an insult to life.'

The cargo had been chilled by the cooling unit in the roof, but now it was warming up. It wasn't the temperature that made Troy shudder, though. 'Is any of it human?'

'I don't know – *yet*. But at least outers and majors aren't endangered. This is worse because some of it's from creatures threatened with extinction.' She waved towards the tiger skins and the horn. 'I'll tell you now, the bones and teeth aren't human.'

Some boxes were not transparent and had lids. Lexi and Troy did not attempt to open them. No doubt, a detailed examination later would reveal yet more bloodshed.

Troy gazed at the eyeballs suspended in some sort of preserving fluid. They almost seemed to be looking back at him, accusing him. He turned away. 'I've seen enough,' he said.

'I'm going to have to analyse an awful lot of DNA to find out where all this stuff came from. Which animals – and animal parts – are here, and whether there's anything human.'

'It's north of horrible.'

'I'll get the Head of Animal Biology to do a visual examination. She'll be able to identify a lot just by looking. That'll speed it up.' Lexi made a brief call. As she clambered out of the vehicle, she muttered, 'I know something that's not here.'

'What?'

'Any sign of humanity.'

Breathing the fresh air again, Troy looked at his partner and said, 'What's it all for, though?'

'Medicine.'

'Medicine?'

'Probably,' Lexi said. 'The superstitious among us – majors – believe in traditional medicine. Quack cures. I'm going to have to do some research, but I remember reading that every part of a tiger can be used in some natural remedy or other.'

'Not all majors think like that,' Troy objected.

'Okay, but some. What's worse, hardly any traditional medicine works. All this killing's for nothing.' She looked down at her life-logger. 'Listen to this. I don't know if any of those brains are from tigers, but an old wives' tale says tiger brain is good for curing laziness and pimples.'

Troy threw up his arms. 'That's shiveringly stupid.'

'Yeah. And powdered rhino horn is supposed to reduce a fever, but it doesn't do as good a job as aspirin, so why not leave the poor rhinos alone?'

Troy nodded.

'What's more,' Lexi said, reading from her online monitor, 'weight-for-weight, powdered rhino horn is the most expensive thing on the planet. A gram costs more than a gram of gold.'

Troy looked across at the unarmed policeman. 'If this van had got a stash of gold, it'd be surrounded by guards with guns,' he said softly.

'That's because people know about gold. They'd take one look at this lot and run in the opposite direction.'

Troy shook his head. 'Somebody's expecting it to arrive somewhere. That person knows what it's worth. How long before they realize something's gone wrong and come looking for it?'

Lexi sighed. 'Okay. One friendly policeman isn't going to fend off a vicious – and bloodthirsty – bunch of animal traffickers for long.' Typing on her life-logger's keypad, she said, 'I'm asking for more back-up.'

When she'd finished, Troy gazed at the van and

the crash site. 'Where do we start? There's so much to test, it's over to you.'

Lexi replied, 'We've got three ways forward – follow up leads on the driver, the van and the cargo.'

'That's a lot for one outer.'

'True. I'll get a whole army of forensic scientists. It'd be too much – and too upsetting – for one person to analyse everything the van's carrying.' She paused before adding, 'For now, I'm going to take a few urgent samples from the cab, the doors and the back, and then get the whole thing wrapped up and moved to the auto section of the labs. It'll be more secure that way. And we can pull it apart bit-by-bit till we get what we need.' She eyed the whole area and asked, 'Thinking about the driver … He – or she – crashed and probably ran off. Where would they go?'

'Not along the road. Too easy to be spotted. He'd take off across the countryside.' On one side of the road, there was a flat agricultural field. On the other, there were some shrubs and cherry trees – and a village in the distance. 'He'd go towards the town,' Troy decided. 'The trees supply a bit of cover and the place – whatever it is – offers transport out of here.'

'Okay. The troops can look for shoeprints over there and quiz people in the town as well.'

Heading in the direction of Shepford, a dark green car with tinted windows slowed menacingly as it neared the incident. It was driverless, so someone inside must have ordered the on-board computer to reduce speed. The passengers were not visible behind the darkened glass, but they were clearly taking a good look at the wreckage. After the car passed, it accelerated down the road. And Troy breathed again.

While Lexi collected microscopic samples of dust – that could include flakes of the driver's skin – and examined every surface for hair and fibres, Troy kept watch. He stood next to the uniformed officer and asked, 'Has anyone else slowed down or stopped?'

The policeman grinned. 'Just about everybody's slowed down. They're nosy. No one's actually stopped.'

'Good,' Troy replied. 'Reinforcements on the way.'

The officer looked puzzled. 'For a crash?'

'For a very valuable cargo.'

A sudden gust of wind blew a blizzard of cherry blossom across the road.

'I haven't looked, but it's just blood and bone, isn't it?'

'Very valuable blood and bone,' Troy said.

A black car suddenly decelerated and cruised past the crime scene.

The policeman nodded in the direction of the quickening car. 'See what I mean?'

Troy nodded.

As Lexi busily gathered samples, Troy felt unsettled. He wasn't quite nervous but, stranded on the side of an isolated road, he felt vulnerable. He suspected that the other two had not thought about how defenceless they were. Every movement caught his eye. In the distance, three male figures were walking towards the village. A farm vehicle was trundling across the agricultural land. A far-off helicopter was beating the air noisily with its rotors. An approaching car maintained power and went past at constant speed, its occupants unconcerned by the accident.

But the next car jammed on its brakes as it drew level with Troy. Brand new and very expensive, it pulled off the road on the same side as the accident. At once, the policeman and Troy stood protectively side-by-side, between the bright green car and the crime scene.

A woman, about forty years of age, leapt out of the passenger's door. When she saw Troy and the police officer, she smiled and held up her hands. 'Florrie Tamsin Two from Animal Biology. Here at the request of Lexi Four.'

Troy relaxed and pointed towards the white van. 'She's over there. Collecting samples.'

In nylon overalls, Lexi came out from behind the wreck. With a grin on her face, she walked towards the biologist. 'Thanks for coming,' she said. Turning towards Troy she added, 'Florrie Two taught me everything I know about animal biology.'

'Not enough,' Florrie replied, 'or you wouldn't have had to drag me out here.'

Lexi laughed. 'Not your fault. It's mine. I specialized in forensics, not biology.'

'From your message, I reckon I'm not going to enjoy this,' Florrie said. 'So, let's get it over with.'

Lexi nodded and told her partner, 'We're going in the back of the van to ID as much stuff as we can.'

'Okay. Give it some welly. I'll let you two get on with it.'

'That means you don't want to see it all again.'

'True. Anyway, I'd only get in the way. I'll stay out here on guard.'

'Huh. Don't tire yourself out.'

Within fifteen minutes, two more vehicles had arrived. A people-carrier brought more back-up and a forensic team. Two majors jumped out of an automatic pick-up truck and glanced around. One of them was wearing overalls displaying her initials: DW. She said, 'Is this the van you want wrapping up and taking to dry dock?'

'Yes,' Troy answered, 'but you'd better wait till two people come out first.'

'OK', DW replied casually. 'Will do. No rush.'

Suddenly, the place had been transformed. It was violated with a variety of officers. That was the effect of crime. It turned a secluded spot into a distasteful hive of activity. It spoiled everything. In the centre of the commotion, Troy felt less exposed but he guessed that this particular crime would be more sickening than most.

SCENE 3

Thursday 15th May, Late afternoon

The woman who found and reported the crashed van lived only five kilometres away. As soon as they'd finished at the crash site, Troy and Lexi went to see her. They had no reason to think of Susannah Appleyard as a suspect, but they needed to speak to her. She had short red hair – a little like Troy's. She was in her thirties and she lived alone.

Troy introduced himself and his partner and then said, 'We're working on the van that crashed up the road. The one you reported.'

'I see.' She screwed up her nose in distaste. 'Not a nice thing to discover.'

'What happened? You drove past and got suspicious?'

'Not suspicious, no. I was concerned that the driver might be hurt. That's why I stopped.'

Troy nodded. 'What did you do exactly?'

'I looked inside to see if anyone was there and needed help.'

'Which parts of the van did you touch?' Lexi asked.

'Er … The driver's door. Nothing else at the front because it was obvious no one was there. I looked underneath, but I don't think I touched anything. Then I went round the back and opened the double-doors.'

'Did you go in?' Troy said.

'You've got to be kidding. There was blood and bone and all sorts. Wild horses wouldn't have dragged me in there. That's when I called the police.'

'Did you see anyone – even in the distance?'

'No. A couple of cars slowed down to take a look, but they didn't stop.'

'Okay,' said Troy. 'Lexi's going to take your fingerprints.'

'Why? I haven't done anything … '

'It's just to eliminate them,' Lexi explained. 'If there are any prints on the van that aren't yours, they'll help us track down who was driving it.'

'You don't know?'

'Not yet,' Lexi replied with a confident smile.

'I wondered if it was driverless – and it'd somehow taken off without its passengers.'

All self-driving vehicles had a failsafe device to stop that happening. With the exception of police cars, the law required at least one person to be in any moving vehicle. The passenger did not have to be a qualified driver, but needed to be capable of instructing the computer in the event of an emergency.

Troy shook his head. 'It was an old model. There was definitely a driver.' He barely paused before asking, 'When you get ill, do you ever try natural medicines?'

Puzzled, Susannah said, 'I take whatever my doctor gives me. Do you mean all that "eye of newt and toe of frog" stuff?'

'If only that was all it was,' Lexi muttered as she helped Susannah roll each fingertip in turn across the screen of her life-logger.

'Yes,' Troy said. 'Traditional medicine.'

'Not that I know of,' Susannah replied. With a

slight shiver, she added, 'And if it involves vans full of body parts, I'll avoid it in the future as well.'

While their car headed for Shepford Crime Central, Troy asked Lexi, 'What was the verdict, then? Did Florrie Two identify all the bits and pieces?'

'Not all, no, but a lot. Most of it came from tigers and black rhinos. In the tubs, she spotted parts from bears, turtles, seahorses and antelope. Possibly the critically endangered saiga antelope. We'll see. DNA analysis will prove it and get the rest.'

'What about those eyes?'

'Tigers'.'

Troy groaned.

'Superstitious majors seem to think that if they eat some part of a powerful animal – like a tiger or rhino – they'll become powerful.'

Troy did not reply straightaway.

Lexi almost exploded. '*You* don't think like that, do you?'

'No, not really,' he said. 'But I can understand why someone might. There's a sort of logic … '

'No, there isn't. Chemistry just doesn't work like that. You're swallowing a bunch of molecules. That's all. The origin of something doesn't have anything to do with the effect it has. I mean, rhino horn! It's just keratin – the same stuff my hair and toenails are made of. Feeling ill? Fancy my crushed toenails?'

'But when the first few heart transplants happened, the patients used to worry whether they'd start to think and act like the donor. So my gran says.'

Scornfully, Lexi asked, 'And did they?'

'No. But it's the same idea. Something could carry over from one living thing to another.'

'Huh. Nothing carries over. The heart's a pump, anyway. It pushes blood around. That's it. Nothing to do with how you act or think.'

'I know, but up *here*,' Troy tapped the side of his head, 'hearts have got tangled up with emotions.'

'Majors are daft. Emotions are formed in the brain, not in a pump. And, even if the heart had got something to do with it, you can only transplant flesh, not feelings.'

Troy smiled. 'You outers do have the uncanny ability to kill romance.'

'And you majors have the uncanny ability to ignore facts.'

'Where have they come from? The animal parts, I mean.'

'Well, they haven't come from zoos around here. I don't think there are that many tigers and rhinos in the country. Anyway, stolen animals would've been big news, and Florrie Two would know all about it as well. No. They've been poached overseas and imported, so there's another angle for us. How did they get into the country? Through an airport? Offloaded from a boat in some secret harbour?'

Troy nodded. 'Talking of other angles … If all this stuff was going into medicines, which doctors are recommending it? Where's it being sold – and who's selling it?'

Lexi was distracted by the vibration of her life-logger. She read the message, put her head in her hands and let out a moan.

'What is it?'

'The pick-up truck hasn't turned up at Crime Central. The drivers have just reported in. They were ambushed by an armed gang. Our crime scene – the van – has been hijacked.'

SCENE 4

Thursday 15th May, Evening

Lexi and Troy did not learn much from the site of the ambush. They didn't learn much from the two majors who'd been forced out of the pick-up truck, either. Neither of them had life-loggers because they weren't police officers. They were support staff. They had been intercepted at a junction by five armed gangsters wearing balaclavas. Four men and one woman, they thought. 'The truck just stopped,' DW said. 'No reason. It just stopped.'

Lexi frowned. 'There's always a reason.'

'I meant there wasn't a fault,' she replied. 'No

obvious reason. And one of the men drove away in it afterwards.'

'That makes the reason pretty obvious,' said Lexi. 'They used an electronic jammer. It put the truck's on-board computer out of action. They dragged you out, turned off the jammer, gave the processor new instructions and – hey presto – off they went.'

'That fits,' Troy agreed. 'But there's a big question.'

Lexi nodded. 'Why has someone stolen our crime scene?' Answering herself, she said, 'Because they didn't want me to do a full analysis.'

'I'm not so sure,' Troy replied. 'We've seen it, photographed it, and you've already taken quite a few samples. It's too late to stop you analysing all that lot.'

'What do you think, then?'

'Maybe they just wanted to reclaim a valuable load. Maybe it's more about keeping a business going than getting rid of evidence.'

'Maybe.'

'But that wasn't the big question,' said Troy

'Oh?'

'Why *here*?' He waved his arm at the junction where the gang had struck. 'How did they know the truck would be here?'

Lexi thought for a moment. 'Human beings make

strange decisions and go by all sorts of different routes. The problem with driverless vehicles is that the computer always plots the same, predictable route.'

'But to predict the way it'd come ... '

'Yeah. They'd need the right start and end points. Then, any direction-finding computer would tell them the route. It'd be easy for them to guess where it was going – Shepford Crime Central – but they must have known the start point: where it crashed.'

'Exactly,' Troy said. 'So who knew?'

'Anyone involved in what we've just done. All the police and forensic science units.'

'The van driver,' Troy added.

'Susannah Appleyard.'

Troy nodded. 'And anyone in those cars that drove past slowly to get a good look.'

SCENE 5

Friday 16th May, Morning

As an outer, Lexi Iona Four did not need sleep. She worked around the clock, but punctuated her days and nights with regular fifteen-minute periods of complete relaxation. While Troy Goodhart slept like a major, Lexi and a small team of forensic scientists analysed the samples she'd salvaged from the smashed van.

'Without the crime scene, there wasn't as much work to get through,' she said to her partner in the morning. 'We tested everything I'd got. There wasn't a scrap of DNA from an outer or a major in the cargo.

So, it's a murder case, but not of human beings. It's murder of endangered animals. All the ones Florrie Two spotted and a few more.'

'Is that really murder?'

'It should be,' she replied. 'It's poaching, illegal trafficking and it's against international law. The Convention on International Trade in Endangered Species of Wild Fauna and Flora – or CITES for short – bans the sale and trade of parts from all threatened wildlife. In my mind, breaking that law is murder.' It was obvious that Lexi's outrage had not faded overnight.

Troy winced as he asked, 'What were those eyeballs going to be used for?'

'Treating epilepsy and malaria.' Lexi shrugged helplessly. 'I could tell you lots. I checked it all out last night. Tiger tails are used in a remedy for skin diseases, their bile – believe it or not – is supposed to be good for convulsions in children with meningitis, and tiger whiskers are taken for toothache. Toothache! And there's plenty more like that. It's ridiculous. Tiger claws are used in sedatives for majors who have trouble sleeping. Perhaps it's their conscience keeping them awake. Crushed tiger bone is supposed to cure just about everything, but easing the pain of arthritis seems to be the main one.'

Troy had heard enough. He changed the subject. 'Any leads on the van driver?'

'I got his DNA from flakes of skin and a tiny bit of blood on the driver's seat. And, hey presto, he's in the DNA database.'

'A bad guy, then.'

'Joe Catchpole. He used to work for a well-known courier company, but they cut back on qualified drivers when their fleet went driverless. He was given an office job instead, but a couple of valuable shipments went to the wrong place.'

'He got the programming wrong?'

'No. He just fancied the goods so he sent them to his own house, forgetting the computer would keep a record.'

'He's not the brightest star in the night sky, is he?'

'If you're talking about brainpower, no. Typical major. But that's one reason he's on our database: theft. He was sacked, spent a bit of time in Shepford Prison, and then set up his own driving business. He's down for a couple of traffic offences as well. Basically, he was driving black-market stuff from importers to suppliers. Doing a courier job that was supposed to be off-radar. No questions asked, no invoices, no official dealings. Just cash.'

'That's what he's still doing.'

Lexi nodded. 'Yeah. We may not have his van any more, but I took its engine number. Confirms Joe Catchpole is the owner. The paint flakes tell me it used to be orange until he sprayed it white. That agrees with the description in the registration.'

'Is he at home?'

'No. I sent some officers to find out. I've got a forensic team looking for any clues he left behind. And I've got Terabyte on standby in case they come across a computer. If there's anything worth finding on it – like a list of all his contacts – Terabyte would find it.'

Terabyte was the nickname of the youngest and best computer geek in Shepford Crime Central. Whenever a case involved electronic media, he would help Lexi and Troy.

Troy smiled. 'I'm not sure if Joe Catchpole's on the run from us or from an angry bunch of traffickers.'

'Now they've got their stock back, maybe they're not so angry.'

'But *he* might not know that. He might be holed up somewhere, scared silly.'

'We'll see.' Lexi paused before she added, 'The team got footprints from the van going in the direction of the town but, after a bit, the trail went cold. In town, a woman thought she saw a man who looked like a photo of Joe Catchpole. He was talking to someone in a green car – through the window. But she wasn't convincing, I'm told. It might have been Catchpole and it might not.'

'What sort of green?' Troy asked. 'Light or dark?'

Lexi shrugged. 'Could've been either. It could've had pink and purple stripes. Her memory wasn't great.'

'Well, I'd be north of surprised if Joe Catchpole was at the sharp end of this case. I bet he wasn't the one who killed and butchered the rhinos. And I don't think he was going to turn them into medicine or sell them. He's probably just a go-between. But I'd still like to speak to him.'

'Yeah.'

'There's something else I want to do. I'm going to go online and blog about my lack of sleep.'

'What lack of sleep?'

'My make-believe lack of sleep. I've tried all the usual cures and nothing works. Insomnia's awful. It's making my life a misery. Is there anyone out there who can help me?'

'Good idea.'

'Maybe someone will offer me tiger claws.'

Lexi nodded. 'Worth a try.'

'I think we should all develop a disease. You can have arthritis.'

'I'm sixteen, like you! Not sixty.'

Troy laughed. 'Use your imagination. God – or evolution, according to you – only gave it to humans. It'd be criminal not to use it. That'd be like a bird refusing to fly.'

'Huh.'

'You'd better be a major as well as old,' Troy said. 'Terabyte can have a fever. One that won't go away.'

Terabyte was an outer, but online he would happily take on the role of a sickly major with a persistent high temperature.

Lexi checked her life-logger for news of the search at Joe Catchpole's house. She shook her head. 'Nothing for Terabyte yet, so – as far as I know – he's not about to be called away. Let's borrow him right now.' She sent him a message.

Terabyte's long and lovable face appeared at the door. His hair flopped forward and he pushed his glasses further up his nose. 'What's cooking?'

Between them, Troy and Lexi brought him up to date with their new case.

'Another weird and not-so-wonderful one.' Terabyte grinned. Always enthusiastic to use his skills, he said, 'Okay. I'm a major and I've got a fever. But that's not all. I'll invent a few identities. They can have anything from itchy skin to cancer.' Starting to type, he added, 'And I'll look for any dodgy sites selling stuff from tigers or whatever, but I don't suppose they do it openly.'

Lexi nodded. 'They probably wrap it up in coded language – or they would have all been arrested by now.'

'I'll see what I can turn up.'

Within an hour, Troy had a response. Someone calling himself – or herself – the Herbal Doctor had reacted to his pleas for help.

HD: *I have natural cure for insomnia. Excellent. You will sleep very very good.*

Troy: *What is it? I've tried all the obvious cures.*

HD: *It is traditional. Very excellent. Many satisfied customers.*

Troy: *What's in it?*

HD: *Natural medicine for the loss of sleeping.*

Troy: *It's expensive.*

HD: *It is effective. Only little needed. Very good.*

Troy: *Is it herbs?*

HD: *No. It has long history of working.*

Troy: *I'm interested. If I call you, will you tell me what it is?*

HD: *Very good. Phone number on site.*

Reading the exchange, Lexi nodded. 'Worth a call.'

'Maybe he doesn't want to admit what he's got in writing, but maybe he'll tell me over the phone.'

Troy: *Please send link to website.*

HD: *I give you instructions.*

When Terabyte examined the directions, he said, 'This is on the dark web. Beyond the reach of most search engines and much loved by underground dealers in this and that.'

Lexi and Troy leaned over his shoulders.

'It's an online store of natural remedies. Loads of plant products. It claims to have a lot of stuff from your hoard as well. See? Fat, bone and all the rest of it from tigers, shark's fin and cartilage, horn from rhinos and saiga antelope.'

'Where is it?' Troy asked.

Terabyte tried the *Contact Me* link.

'No physical location,' Terabyte replied with a crooked grin. 'Just an email address and a mobile phone number. Very handy.'

'All right. I'll make a call,' Troy said.

'If you want to know where this Herbal Doctor is, I'll trace it.'

'Yeah. Give it some welly.'

Troy put the conversation on loudspeaker so that Lexi and Terabyte could listen. The voice that answered belonged to a middle-aged man. His accent told them he was from the Far East.

'Yes,' he said. 'Insomnia. Good ancient cure.'

'But what is it? I like to know what I'm taking.'

'I make it now. My mother make it before me. Before that, my grandmother. Many generations. More than a thousand years. Excellent.'

Terabyte worked quickly at his keypad, triangulating the position of the man's mobile phone and hopefully his black-market business.

'How does it work?'

'It soothes the mind. It eases into sleep. From an animal that sleeps well.'

'A lion?'

'No.'

'I've heard about tiger-claw remedies – and there's a lot about tigers on your website. Is that what it is?'

'You buy it, yes?'

Clearly, the Herbal Doctor did not want to incriminate himself by revealing his illegal ingredients, even though his shop front on the dark web was more explicit. Perhaps he was worried that Troy was recording the conversation.

'Yes,' Troy answered. 'I see the buy button on my computer. I can pay you now but I want the cure straightaway. Where are you? I'll come and collect it.'

'I mail only. No shop here.'

'But … '

'I mail it quickly. Just for you. You become satisfied customer. Good sleeps.'

Troy glanced at Terabyte and raised his eyebrows. Terabyte replied silently by putting up both thumbs.

'Okay. Thanks,' Troy said.

The call ended abruptly.

'Yes,' Terabyte said. 'You're in luck. It's a farm not far from Shepford. I've pinned it down to an area of about three square metres inside one of the buildings.'

'Good stuff.' Troy grabbed his coat.

Lexi grimaced. 'Strange farm. What do they breed? Tigers, rhinos, sharks?'

'Program a car for us and send the details to our life-loggers, please,' Troy said to Terabyte. 'We're on our way.'

Lexi strode out of the room with her partner. 'All over by lunchtime?' she said with a wry grin.

SCENE 6

Friday 16th May, Late morning

It looked like a conventional farm. Dairy cattle on one side of the track leading to a collection of buildings, and sheep in the field on the other side. The whole place was dotted with machinery and tatty outbuildings. There was no sign of a pick-up truck or a crippled white van, but they could easily be hidden in one of the shacks. The farmyard was a quadrangle enclosed by an old sprawling house, a barn, a cattle shed and workshop. Chickens ranged freely, pecking at the ground, uninterested in the two visitors. A collie was much more concerned and protective. It didn't attack or even go close to the detectives, but it barked loud warnings. Two ginger cats strolled across the messy courtyard with barely a glance at Troy and Lexi. Beyond the workshop was a large pond. The surface water rippled with feeding fish.

A farmhand appeared from the cattle shed with a stun-gun in his hand. It was the type used for putting large animals to sleep.

Sensing danger, Troy called out, 'We're detectives and everything that happens here is being filmed and sent to Shepford Crime Central.'

'What do you want?' the young man growled.

'I want to speak to the person who sells traditional medicines. The Herbal Doctor.'

'Look around. We're a farm, not a hospital.'

'Then why has he just taken a call in that building?' Troy nodded towards the workshop.

The man holding the stun-gun shook his head. 'You've got it all wrong. Bad mistake. It's not here. Get back in your car and go away.'

'We'll just see what's in your workshop.'

'No, you won't.'

'But you invited us to look around.'

'No, I didn't.'

'Sorry, but you did. You gave us permission a few

seconds ago.' He tapped his life-logger. 'I have it on record.'

Next to him, Lexi whispered, 'Nice – but risky.'

'No way. Turn round and leave right now.'

While they made their way towards the door, the man with the stun-gun sprinted angrily towards them. At once, Lexi stepped in front of Troy. She assumed a sidewise high stance, feet planted firmly apart for stability. When the farmhand took a swipe at her with the gun, she swayed to one side, dodged the blow, and felled him with a knife-hand strike to the neck followed by a knock-out punch to the left side of his forehead. He crumpled to the ground and Lexi kicked the stun-gun away.

The door to the workshop opened and an older man appeared. He glanced with horror at the figure lying on the ground and immediately launched a pitchfork like a javelin straight at Lexi.

Helpless, Troy screamed a warning, 'Lexi!'

She turned and, adrenalin pumping, lurched away from the missile. Her left hand shot out and caught the shaft mid-flight. Raising it high over her head, she jabbed it down at the farmhand's right leg. It was a perfect shot. Two of the pitchfork's prongs jabbed into the earth either side of his ankle, pinning him to the ground.

She extracted from her pocket two plastic hand ties but hesitated before using them on either of the two men. Snarling, the collie came towards her. Taking up another pose, ready to strike, she stared into its eyes, waiting.

The dog came to a halt. Somehow, it recognized a superior fighter and backed sheepishly away.

Lexi strode towards the older man in the doorway. 'Clever dogs, collies.' She spun him around and cuffed his hands behind his back. 'Cleverer than attempting to murder a police officer.'

Then she went back to the unconscious farmhand. While she secured his wrists with the second plastic tie, she smiled because a chicken had taken the opportunity to peck at his boots.

'All right,' Troy said to the older man. 'Tell us your names.'

'I am Quang Xuan. He is my son, Rufus Quang. Have you hurt him?'

'No,' Lexi replied. 'I hardly touched him. He'll come round in a few minutes.'

'So, Quang is your family name?' Troy asked.

'Yes. I am from Vietnam. I marry here.'

'You're the Herbal Doctor?'

Shyly, he nodded.

'Let's go in,' Troy said, opening the workshop door.

The inside of the well-lit building was a cross between a laboratory, a pet shop and a plant nursery. There was a bench with scales, pestles and mortars, scalpels, bottles of chemicals, blenders, saws and a variety of other tools and devices. Near the door, there was a chair and a computer. On the opposite wall were two long rows of cages. Some were empty and others contained small animals like mice, cats and birds. At the far end of the building, exotic plants were growing under ultraviolet lights. On one side, there were some large fish tanks.

Lexi stood beside a cabinet. Its drawers were labelled with intricate and beautiful Vietnamese words. She ran her life-logger over the labels and requested a translation.

'What exactly do you do here?' Troy asked.

'Prepare medicines. All good.'

'From plants, animals and fish?'

'Yes.'

'What do you keep in the pond outside?'

'Carp.'

'You breed carp?'

'Yes.'

'For making medicine?'

'Yes.'

On hearing a car, Lexi peered outside. Rufus had regained consciousness and was using his left leg to kick at the pitchfork, desperately trying to free his right ankle. But he wasn't going to make it in time. Alerted by the detectives' transmissions, four uniformed officers had arrived and were about to arrest the young farmer.

'Your page on the dark web talks about tigers, rhinos and sharks.' Troy held out his arms. 'You don't have enough room for them here.'

Xuan swallowed and looked down at the floor. 'We import. Tigers from Vietnam and Malaysia. All on sale at Hanoi Airport. Bones, skin and many parts. Rhino horn and shark fin and cartilage from the east also.'

Consulting Xuan's website on her life-logger, Lexi said, 'You prepare tiger brain to treat pimples and laziness.'

'Very good cure.'

'Can you show me a brain? An actual brain. Not the powder.'

Xuan went to a cupboard and nodded towards it, unable to use his bound hands. 'Shelf in centre.'

Lexi opened it up and brought out a sealed box, very similar to some of the containers in the white van. She peeled back the lid carefully and revealed a whole brain in preserving fluid. Examining it, she said, 'It looks small.'

'Yes,' the Herbal Doctor replied. 'Young tiger have best brain.'

'When were you last in contact with Joe Catchpole?' Troy asked.

'I have no knowledge of this person.'

A police officer appeared in the doorway and asked, 'All under control?'

'Yes,' Troy replied. 'Arrest Rufus Quang – the one outside – for attempted assault. This is Quang Xuan. Attempted murder.'

'And offences against the Convention on the International Trade in Endangered Species,' Lexi added with venom.

'You can take him now as well,' said Troy. 'I'll question him later in Crime Central. But can you get some of your people to search the farm for a white van and one of our pick-up trucks?'

'Will do.'

Lexi sent a message, requesting a team of helpers from Forensics. She also hoped that Florrie Tamsin Two was available. Surrounded by quackery and cruelty, she shook her head and said to her partner, 'No one's going to hijack this crime scene. Lots of

DNA for profiling. I want to see if some of this stuff matches the samples from the van. If they do – hey presto – it's all over. Our fastest ever case. But … '

'What?'

'Let's wait for the results.'

SCENE 7

Friday 16th May, Lunchtime

'In a way,' Lexi said, 'it's a sweet and sour meal.' She fingered a jumbo prawn that was encrusted with black ants. 'The prawn's sweet and the formic acid in the ants is sour. They give you a real kick. Great combination.'

Troy smiled wistfully. 'Sweet and sour. Major and outer. You and me.'

Externally, majors and outers looked much the same, but internally they were very different. Outers ate a diet based on insects, and their metabolism did not convert alcohol into intoxicating substances.

Lexi knocked back some cider. 'Five-and-a-bit weeks we've been together. I've saved your skin once or twice and you've saved mine. We've solved all three cases. I thought you'd be rubbish but … '

'Another good combination?'

'If we crack this one as well, yeah.'

'I don't trust Xuan,' said Troy. 'I think he was lying about getting the tigers from Vietnam and Malaysia. Too much hesitation and too little eye contact.'

'I checked online. He was right that you can buy tiger parts at Hanoi Airport. He wasn't lying about that.'

Troy shrugged. 'Maybe his body language is different, hard to read. Even so … '

'I'm not convinced yet either. But I want more facts and less gut reaction.'

'Sweet and sour.'

'Huh.'

'Okay,' said Troy. 'I won't question Quang Xuan till tomorrow – after you've done a full sweep of the farm and got more evidence.'

'Agreed.'

'How are your team getting on at Joe Catchpole's place? You would have said something if they'd found a killer clue.'

'They've got nothing that links him to anyone

suspicious. No record of repeated trips. Nothing linking him with a gang. No dead tigers. Definitely no computer and no mobile phone.'

Troy sighed. 'Nothing for Terabyte to get his teeth into.' He took a forkful of meat and potato pie with lashings of brown sauce.

With a frown, Lexi watched him eating the mush. 'The most hi-tech item was a notepad.'

'What was on it?'

'Nothing. So, I got them to give it to the documents section. They'll find out what he wrote by visualizing impressions.'

'You mean, looking for writing that shows through from the last piece he tore off?'

She nodded. 'ESDA. Electrostatic Detection Apparatus. It picks out tiny dents in paper. Maybe it'll be the name of whoever was paying him to do the job. Or the address he was getting the body parts from – or taking them to. Or maybe it'll just be the name of a nice place to eat.' She savoured another jumbo prawn and then added, 'The dealers must have got in touch with him somehow – to organize the pick-up and delivery.'

'A mobile phone call?'

'Yeah. But how did they know he was up for some dodgy delivering in the first place? Their paths must have crossed somehow, somewhere. I'm getting a list of everyone who was in Shepford Prison at the same time as Catchpole.' She shrugged. 'Maybe that's when our bad guys and Joe Catchpole met each other.'

Both of their life-loggers vibrated with the same incoming message. Neither a white van nor a police pick-up truck had been found on the Quangs' land.

They finished their lunches and went back to the farm. Troy interviewed the rest of the Quang family – Xuan's wife and his younger son and daughter – but they seemed to have little to do with the Herbal Doctor's business. They also seemed to have no knowledge of Joe Catchpole, a white van with a gruesome load, and an official pick-up truck.

Florrie Tamsin Two had not turned up. While a crime-scene team went about its meticulous searches, Lexi concentrated on the contents of the drawers of the cabinet. She took and bagged a small sample of every remedy. She concentrated on those that could have been made from the white van's cargo. She would first profile the DNA in preparations labelled as rhino horn, antelope horn, and tiger bone, brain and eyeballs.

She interrupted her work only to read a message

from the specialists in document analysis. Looking paler than normal, she said to Troy, 'It's the result on Joe Catchpole's pad. The impression's a bit patchy but it's easy enough to make out what he scribbled.'

'Which was?'

She seemed reluctant to reveal the result – as if she could not believe it. She shook her head and sighed. 'He wrote down Florrie Tamsin Two's name and address. Actually, he made a mistake and wrote *Tasmin*. But it's still Florrie because he got her work address right.'

Troy gazed at his partner. 'I see why you're bothered. Your favourite animal biologist. But remember we've got a witness who may have seen Joe Catchpole talking to someone in a car that may have been Florrie Two's posh green one.'

'Too many may haves.'

'Yes. But worth mentioning.' Troy paused before adding, 'And there's the hijack of the van. Whoever organized it knew where it crashed and where it was going. Florrie Two ticks that box as well – whether she met up with Joe Catchpole or not.'

Lexi shook her head again. 'I don't see why Florrie would have anything to do with this horrid trade. She hates it.'

'But you believe in facts.' Turning the tables on his

partner, Troy said, 'You can't ignore them because they don't fit with your instinct.'

'I know.' She took a deep breath and said, 'I'm going back to the lab to crack on with my main samples. The team can finish off here without me.'

SCENE 8

Lexi had loaded all of her high-priority samples from the farm into the DNA sequencer. She had meditated for just over fifteen minutes and now she was waiting with Troy and Terabyte in the computer room for the results. It would be a few hours before the tests were complete.

One of Terabyte's online personas had attracted the attention of someone with a username of Nat Med. 'It's a really vile one,' Terabyte said. 'Nat Med is going to cure me of cancer with shark cartilage. It's rubbish. I checked. It comes from the belief that sharks don't get cancer – but they do.'

Troy let out a sigh. 'I don't know how they can give people false hope, promising a cure with stuff that won't make any difference. That's north of immoral.'

'It's just taking money off desperate people,' Terabyte replied. 'Desperate and desperately ill.'

'It's more than that,' said Lexi. 'It's pushing endangered animals to the brink of extinction as well.' She examined her own computer and exclaimed, 'Hey. The same blogger's telling me I can fix arthritis and depression with rhino horn. And drinking his tiger bone wine will ease the pain of my arthritis.'

'I wonder if he'd take these things if *he* had cancer or arthritis,' Troy murmured. 'Or whether he'd just go into hospital.'

Lexi smiled. 'Good question. I wish I could ask him – or her. Or them.' She turned towards Terabyte. 'Well? Have you got in there and worked out who Nat Med is?'

'The site's anonymous and well protected, but I'm working on it.'

Lexi left him to hack into the web address while she checked on the progress of her forensic tests. She also examined all of the tyre impressions she'd recorded at the Quangs' farm. None of them matched her photograph of the white van's tyres. Then she began the long process of reading the criminal records of every inmate whose time in prison overlapped with Joe Catchpole's. Hoping to find someone who was inside for medical fraud, animal cruelty or a similar crime, she entered each one into a spreadsheet: name, offence, time served and dates in prison.

Her indignation – and bouts of meditation – kept her going as the afternoon became evening, Crime Central emptied of weary majors, evening became night, and eventually night gave way to dawn.

SCENE 9

Lexi was wearing an expression of wry amusement and frustration.

'How's it gone?' asked Troy.

'Xuan Quang's cures are counterfeit. They don't work and they're not what he says they are.'

Puzzled, Troy said, 'What are they?'

'The bits of tiger are actually domestic cats. That's why the brain was small. It was a cat's. His rhino horn is human fingernails and toenails with a little extra calcium and phosphorus chucked in. His shark products are from other fish, mainly carp. That's that. End of lead.'

Troy nodded slowly. 'I thought he was lying about importing animal parts. He didn't want to admit his powdered rhino horn was ground up human nails.'

Lexi laughed. A sad laugh. 'Human nails will do the same job as rhino horn. Cats' whiskers are as good as tigers'. Powdered carp's fin is a pretty good substitute for shark.' She shrugged. 'They're all useless. They're all fake medicine.'

'So, his farm really is a farm. He breeds animals to take the place of tigers and the like. You should be pleased he hasn't killed any wild animals.'

'I am – but it's still a rotten scam.' She scanned his list of crackpot cures. 'His crime's about trade descriptions – fraud – but … Tiger, cat. Horn, nail. Biologically, it's a fine line.'

Troy agreed. 'Let's pass him to someone else. It's not our baby.'

'But he still tried to take my head off with a pitchfork.'

'He didn't stand a chance against you.'

'Maybe not, but he still tried. It's all on video.'

'Let's pass that up to the chief as well. We're witnesses, not investigators.'

'All right,' Lexi replied. 'Because I want to get on with the real thing. We're no nearer the bad guys.'

Gazing at his partner, Troy said, 'You know what we've got to do now.'

Lexi sighed. 'I suppose.'

'See Florrie Tamsin Two.'

'Yeah. I'm not looking forward to it.'

Before they set out, though, Terabyte came to see them. At once, his face told them that he was proud of his latest endeavours.

'You're looking smug,' Lexi said. 'You must have hacked in and identified Nat Med.'

'I didn't actually,' he replied. 'Solid defences. Even I have my limits.'

'So … '

Terabyte flicked his hair behind his ears. 'I used a bit of logic and intelligence. Four months ago, there was a man on the site with a username of BarnCraft. He said – well, he blogged – that he'd been given three months to live by his doctor. Lung cancer. Nat Med prescribed shark cartilage. That won't have fixed anything so, assuming his doctor was somewhere near right, I went through death certificates for the last two months. I filtered out anything that wasn't a male adult major. That's still a depressing number of deaths. I ditched all the certificates that didn't mention lung cancer. That gave me a manageable number. And I found Barney Woodcraft. BarnCraft? Barney Woodcraft? Coincidence? I don't think so.'

'Nice work,' Troy said.

'Oh, I haven't finished. I fished around in databases. Barney Woodcraft is – was – married. His wife's Madeline and she's still alive, living down south in Pullover Creek. I thought you might want to set up a call – to see if her husband tried shark cartilage – so I found her number. I sent it to your computer.'

'Very nice work.' Troy thanked Terabyte, glanced at the clock and said, 'It's early but maybe not too early. I'll try a video call.'

It took two attempts but Troy soon found himself looking at Madeline Woodcraft's worn face on his monitor. 'I'm sorry to bother you. I'm Detective Troy Goodhart of Shepford Crime Central and I'm investigating fake traditional medicines. Looking through the files I've got here, I see that your husband, Barney, might have tried a natural remedy for lung cancer. Would you be willing to help me?'

Madeline gazed back at him. 'Go on.'

'First, I'm very sorry to hear what happened to Barney. You have my sympathy.'

Madeline blinked. A slight nod of her head acknowledged his condolences.

'Did he buy any natural cures online?'

'Shark cartilage. We were told sharks don't get cancer. They have natural immunity. Something in their cartilage wards it away.'

'Do you know if that's true?' Troy asked.

'At the time we didn't. We accepted it. It sounded … reasonable. And we wanted to believe. I checked after Barney … Anyway, it's nonsense.'

Troy nodded. 'So, you think Barney was conned.'

'Yes.'

Troy was pleased to hear the disdain in Madeline's voice and see it in her expression. It meant that she'd do everything in her power to help his case. 'Who did you buy it from?'

'Someone calling himself Nat Med.'

'Yes. I've come across him – or her. He's in my sights. But do you know who he really is?'

'No.'

'When the cartilage arrived, was there a note in with it? Anything more about the person or organization that sent it?'

'No. Just a recommended way of taking the powder.'

'Do you have any left?'

'No.'

'What about the wrapping? Did you keep it by any chance?'

'Sorry. I'm not helping. I want to, but … '

'Did you pay electronically?'

'Yes. I had a look at the bank statement. The money wasn't transferred to a named person or company. It was just some reference number.'

'You don't have to send me the details because it's private to you and Barney but, if you want to give me a better chance of catching people like Nat Med, you could email them to me.'

Madeline sniffed. 'I'll do that. Anything to stop him preying on other people.'

'Thank you. One last thing. When you opened the package, did you note where it had come from?'

'Oh. Yes. I meant to say. It was where you are. The postmark was Shepford.'

Troy nodded and smiled. 'That's very helpful. Thanks.'

SCENE 10

'Sorry I couldn't be with you yesterday,' Florrie said. 'Work, you understand. Did you make any headway?'

'Not really,' Lexi answered. 'We ruled out one farm. Not what you'd call a massive breakthrough.'

The biologist was standing in her well-equipped research laboratory. Long lights suspended from the ceiling illuminated plants growing in plastic trays and five watery tanks that mimicked pond life. The containers lay side-by-side on a wide bench and water flowed into them from dangling transparent tubes. At one end of the bench, there were three aquariums and lab coats hung from hooks on the wall. At the other was a chair, a computer terminal and a sink. Above it, glassware was drying on heated upward-pointing spikes.

Florrie was wearing classy designer clothes and luxury shoes. Her hair and make-up were immaculate. Everything about her suggested poise and wealth.

Troy took over the conversation. 'What's your opinion of natural cures?'

She shrugged. 'That's too big – too general – a question.' She waved a hand towards the green shoots in one of the plastic trays. 'Some plants have a real effect on human metabolism and relieve symptoms. Some only work in outers, some only in majors. Either way, nature sometimes does better than chemists making medicines in labs. Sometimes, though, chemists are as good as nature. There's an acid in bear bile that dissolves gall stones, but there's no need to torture bears to get it because chemists have made the same acid in the lab. Then there's the rest of the traditional medicine business. This is where chemists are much better than nature.' She sighed wearily. 'The vast majority of it is plain kooky – including all the so-called remedies from threatened species. The people behind it like to give explanations for how it works – eat part of a strong animal and you'll gain strength – because they want it to sound scientific. It isn't science. It's pseudo-science. It's completely bogus. It should be discouraged and despised.'

To Troy, her delivery sounded more like a lecture than a chat. He wondered if, as a lecturer, she'd adopted a familiar style so she could come across as genuine. He tried to knock her off-balance. 'How does Joe Catchpole fit into all this?' he asked.

'Who?'

'Joe Catchpole.'

'That sounds like something you'd ask a suspect. Am I under some sort of suspicion?' Her eyes went from Troy to Lexi.

Lexi looked away.

'Do you know him?' said Troy.

'No.'

'Here's a picture.' Troy held up his life-logger. 'Have you seen him before?'

'No.'

'Have you ever spoken to him?'

'No.'

'He's a driver.'

'Of the white van, by any chance?'

'Yes.'

'Nothing to do with me,' Florrie claimed. 'Ask Lexi. She knows I'd never … '

'Can you tell me, then, why he wrote your name and address on a piece of paper?'

Taken aback, Florrie hesitated. 'Er … No. I can't. That's. … strange, to say the least. No idea.'

SCENE 11

With a beer in her hand, Lexi studied her monitor and then looked up at Troy. 'That bright blue colour's been bugging me. The scuff mark on the side of the van: I was sure I'd seen it before. Not long back. So I looked over our last case with my life-logger on fast forward. Guess what I saw.'

'Something bright blue?'

'The squirrel farm in Pickling. We never went to it, but we saw its flag flying. See?'

Troy peered at the screen. 'It fits. Like a thousand other things, it's the same blue.'

'I've been on the company's website. It's their corporate colour. The logo, the interior walls, the product packaging. All bright blue.'

'You want to go there to get a sample?'

Lexi nodded. 'It's the only way. Microscopic examination and chemical analysis will tell me if it's the same paint as the stuff I scraped off the van.'

'Okay.'

'And we need to look for a white mark as well. If our van was there and it grazed against something blue, it'd leave a tell-tale smudge of paint. Every contact leaves a trace.'

Troy smiled. 'Now you're pushing your luck.'

'Huh. If the blues match, I'll go over every square millimetre that's near enough to a road to be hit by a van.'

'I know you will. Methodically.'

'Yeah. I haven't finished with the van just because someone's nicked it.'

With a pained expression, Troy said, 'When do you want to go?'

Troy's father had died in Pickling only eight days earlier. Lexi knew it would be a harrowing trip for her partner, but she was keen to make a start. She looked at him sympathetically. 'Now?'

Troy took a deep breath. 'Now's as good – or as bad – as any other time.'

In the car, Troy asked, 'How's that list going? The one with everybody who was in prison with Joe Catchpole.'

'My spreadsheet's not highlighting any links that need looking into.'

Troy thought about it for a moment and then said, 'Don't forget that prisoners aren't the only ones in a prison.'

Lexi nodded. 'I'm going to add the guards and service staff to the data.'

'Remember when we talked to Dominic Varney in our second case?'

'Yeah. The undercover detective.'

'I know he was in a different prison, but he talked about the governor bringing in a vet for his dogs.'

'Okay. Good point. Visitors. Especially medical ones. A vet or a doctor.'

'It'd be good to find out what sort of thing the Shepford Prison doctor prescribes for sick inmates.'

'And whether Joe Catchpole got ill,' Lexi added.

'Exactly.'

'I'll work on it – after a meditation.'

Before they reached Pickling, Lexi had the information they needed. Early in his prison stay, Joe Catchpole had been diagnosed with food poisoning. Dr Henry Patrick Fifteen had supervised his treatment.

Wasting no time, Troy introduced himself to the governor of Shepford Prison by phone. 'Tell me about Dr Henry Patrick Fifteen,' he said.

'He does what's necessary.'

Tetchy, Troy asked, 'What's that supposed to mean?'

'Look,' the governor replied with a sigh. 'How can I put this diplomatically? Not many doctors are keen to do regular prison visits, so we don't necessarily get the best. Top doctors are popular – fully booked with law-abiding patients. What a surprise. They don't have time to fix our guys as well. Some would say that's how it should be. Maybe inmates don't deserve the best.'

'They're human beings, aren't they?'

'I didn't say that was my opinion. Some people think we look after them too well. They believe a good doctor is a luxury that criminals should forfeit.'

'You're not impressed with Henry Fifteen.'

'I didn't say that either. I'm very grateful he comes to us but, no, he isn't always able to help.'

'What sort of thing does he prescribe?'

'Look. He doesn't tell me how to run the prison and I don't interfere with his surgeries.'

While Troy was speaking to the governor of Shepford Prison, the car went past Pickling Prison. The rear of the bleak building was covered with scaffolding as builders repaired fire damage.

His mood going downhill rapidly, Troy lost patience. 'All right. I'll go and see him. Don't tell him, though.'

Troy looked outside for a while and then turned towards Lexi. 'I think Terabyte should build me a life under another name. Trent Goodall. My medical record should show repeated bouts of severe insomnia.'

'You're going to present yourself to Henry Fifteen as sleepy Trent Goodall?'

'Exactly.'

The squirrel farm was one large brick building and several outhouses. Just about every surface apart from the brickwork was painted in the same striking colour. Bright blue was clearly the corporate visual identity. Lorries entered the site and veered off to the left side of the main building to the goods entrance. Cars and smaller vehicles approaching the farm went along a private lane and parked in front of the main entrance. They were close to the areas painted blue but not close enough to have an accidental scrape.

On the left of the factory, beyond the tarmac, there was a small wood. As if to blend with the corporate colour, it had a rich blanket of bluebells.

Lexi hunted for signs of damage near the side entry. She found two dents in a blue guard-rail, but neither showed evidence of white paint. She guessed that they'd been caused by the farm's own trucks. The HGVs were mostly the same blue colour, so any careless reversing would not leave behind traces of a different colour. Disappointed, Lexi took flecks of the blue paint from several outside surfaces and put them securely in evidence bags.

Inside the main building, Troy asked the manager, 'Do you have any white vans in your fleet?'

He smiled. 'No. Everything's blue. It drives me mad, but it's a large part of our identity.' He shrugged. 'People know us by it.'

'Do you deal with any animals apart from squirrels?'

'The factory used to slaughter cattle for beef, but I took us in a different direction. We're completely specialized. This country's biggest and best provider of free-range squirrel meat. We're not going to dilute that image – and our reputation – by expanding into other products.'

Troy held up his life-logger for the manager to see the screen. 'Joe Catchpole. Have you ever seen him or had anything to do with him?'

'Not that I recall.'

'Do you have lots of security cameras?'

'Only in a few strategic places – mainly to keep an eye on squirrel behaviour.'

'Do you monitor vehicles coming and going?'

'No,' the manger answered. 'I can't help you with that.'

'Okay. Thanks.'

Troy decided to give up. He was eager to get out of Pickling. He hadn't heard or seen anything remotely suspicious. He thought they were wasting time.

The driverless car cruised smoothly back down the farm lane. Just before it reached the main road, though, it went through the main gate and Lexi shouted, 'Stop here!'

'What's up?' Troy asked with a sigh.

Already on her way out of the door, Lexi said, 'The gatepost.'

It was the familiar bright blue. There was no sign of damage on the nearside post but, when Lexi examined the one on the right of the lane, she broke into a smile. Pointing with her gloved left hand, she said, 'That's what I've come for.'

There was a definite mark where something white had brushed against the gatepost. Using a small sharp knife, Lexi sliced a section of the damaged paintwork into a transparent evidence bag and sealed it. Then, looking at the paint flake with a magnifying glass, she muttered, 'Hey presto. Under the white layer, it's orange.'

'That's … '

'Significant,' she said. 'I need a full analysis to confirm it, but I'm confident. Our van was here.'

They got back into the car and Lexi instructed the computer to take them to Pickling Crime Central. She wanted to use a forensic laboratory and she was too impatient to wait until they got back to Shepford.

'There weren't any bits of squirrel in the back of the van, were there?' Troy asked as soon as the car began its short journey.

'No.'

'They're a long way south of endangered. The grey ones are pests that get everywhere.'

'Including majors' dinner plates, yeah,' said Lexi. 'I don't know what the connection is with our case, but I'm pretty sure there is one.'

SCENE 12

Saturday 17th May, Late afternoon

Chemical analysis had confirmed what Lexi suspected. The white paint smudged on one of the squirrel farm's gateposts was identical to the van's. The orange layer made it particularly distinctive. Lexi also proved that the blue paint collected from the side of the white van was identical in colour and composition to the paint used on the gate of the Pickling squirrel factory. Her results meant a return trip to the farm.

Troy sighed as they entered the main building again and walked towards the reception. 'I can't tell you how much I hate Pickling.'

Lexi smiled wryly. 'You don't have to. I can tell – even though I'm not the perceptive one.'

They were escorted to the manager's bright blue office by a receptionist wearing a bright blue uniform. Wearing a bright blue tie, the man behind the desk looked up at his familiar guests and said, 'Back again?'

Of course, his question was unnecessary. Troy believed he was covering up nerves with phony cheerfulness. Troy showed him a picture of the white van and said, 'We can prove this van came onto your site.'

'When?'

'We don't know. It might have been quite recently.'

The manager shrugged.

'Have you seen it here?'

He smiled unconvincingly. 'Everyone's seen a white van – they're common enough – but, no, not here.'

'Can you account for it being here?'

'I can't rule out – I don't know – electricians or plumbers coming to fix a fault, or something like that.'

'I can,' Troy said. 'It's something to do with animals.'

The manager shook his head. 'No idea, then.'

From the office window, Troy could see the factory floor where the squirrel meat was prepared. 'One of your production lines is much bigger than the others.'

'That's where the cattle were processed. It'll be replaced soon.'

'Is this a twenty-four hour operation?'

'No. We'll be shutting down for the day soon. Almost everyone here is a major – that reflects the nature of the food – so we close at night. And all day tomorrow.'

Troy exchanged a glance with his partner.

'I need a list of everyone who works here. With a description of what they do.'

'No problem,' he replied. 'I'll get it sent.'

On their own in an interview room at the squirrel factory, Troy looked at Lexi and said, 'How many – and what sort of – people are we after?'

'How do you mean?'

'I reckon there'll be at least four in the chain. Maybe more. There's the importer. If the animals arrive whole – sedated or dead – or even in big chunks, there'll be a vet or someone to cut them up.'

'A butcher, maybe.'

'Yes, a butcher. Then there's Joe Catchpole who takes the bits to the next link in the chain. That's whoever turns the parts into medicines. After that, someone sells them and maybe a doctor dishes them out.'

'Some of those might be the same person. A doctor might prepare the cures, prescribe and sell them.'

'Yes,' Troy agreed, 'but which one's most likely to work at a squirrel farm?'

'A vet or a butcher.'

'Exactly,' said Troy. 'I imagine that's who we're after.'

Lexi consulted the list of staff. 'No vet. They probably call one in when they need it. But they've got five butchers.'

'Not too many to talk to ... '

Lexi interrupted. 'First, let me take a few swabs when they stop work. If one of them's been moonlighting – butchering tigers and the like – I'll find something. No matter how well they wipe down afterwards, they can't wash away every trace of blood, fur, skin or whatever. I'll find it in the cracks and crevices.'

Troy nodded. 'I can see how it could work. At night, after the farm shuts down, a new batch of carcasses arrives. The butcher does his – or her – worst and the bits go in Joe Catchpole's van for delivery to Shepford.'

'Not much light, so Catchpole grazes the gatepost with his van on the way in or out.'

'Yeah. All done before dawn – before the staff turn up for the next day.'

'We'll see,' said Lexi. 'I'll get those samples. Mainly from where they dealt with cows. It's big enough to handle our victims.'

'Give it plenty of welly – in case they scrub down like crazy afterwards.'

Lexi waved a cotton bud at him. 'No match for me. If need be, I'll wait till it's dark and spray with luminol but, in a meat factory, that might detect blood almost everywhere. I'll probably just take loads of samples from the nooks and crannies that are hard to clean.' She paused before adding, 'I know. I'll get into the U-bends under the sinks and sample the gunge. If somebody's swilled non-squirrel bits away, there'll be a few scraps of skin or hair caught in the drain.'

Troy turned up his nose. 'Rather you than me.'

SCENE 13

Loading her fifteenth sample into the automated DNA sequencer in Pickling Crime Central, Lexi looked across at her partner. 'It's after eleven, you know.'

'I know.' But Troy was refusing to sleep. 'Tonight I'm living like an outer.'

Lexi sighed. 'You'll be grumpy in the morning.'

'Fair enough.'

'You're a major. You need to spend a third of your life asleep. If you don't, you'll get tired, grouchy and forgetful. Your concentration and attention span will disappear. I looked all this up when I was young – and curious about majors. The parts of your brain that control language, planning, judgement and memory will more or less shut down.'

'I know.'

'Ah!' Lexi cried. 'Got it! You're preparing yourself for the role of a patient with insomnia.'

'I want to look the part.'

Lexi laughed. 'You're a method actor.'

'I need to look convincing. That's all.'

'And, while you do it, I've got to put up with a worn-out, bad-tempered, scatter-brained partner.'

'We all have to make sacrifices.'

'Huh.'

Lexi finished loading all of the samples from the squirrel farm. 'That's done,' she said. 'They'll take care of themselves till morning. We can go out, grab some bugs and a few bottles of beer, and join all the outers dancing the night away.'

Troy suppressed a weary groan.

SCENE 14

Sunday 18th May, Morning

Speechless, the manager of the squirrel farm fiddled nervously with his car keys and stared blankly at the two young detectives. Troy had requested a meeting with him at the factory, even though it was closed on a Sunday. Perhaps that was why he wasn't wearing anything bright blue. On his day off, the manager was having a break from the company's colour.

Troy told him the results of the overnight forensic tests and then waited, allowing silence to amplify the tension.

Eventually, the manager cleared his throat and murmured, 'Tiger and antelope?'

'Yes,' Troy said. 'Most of the DNA was from the drain.'

Lexi looked down at the empty factory floor and added, 'You call it Station 4. The big one, designed for cows, you told us yesterday.'

Prickly, Troy asked, 'How do you explain that?'

'I … er … I don't. I can't. It's … '

'What?'

'I was going to say it's impossible, but … ' He sighed. 'I don't suppose … '

Troy shook his head. 'No. It's not a mistake. The result's very clear.'

'One hundred per cent,' Lexi said.

At last, the manager put down the keys and fidgeted instead with one of the buttons of his shirt. 'It's a mystery. Squirrels, yes. But anything else? No. I can't … ' He shrugged helplessly.

Troy believed his anxiety and bewilderment were genuine, but Troy's judgement was suffering through lack of sleep. 'Which of your butchers normally works at Station 4? Is it always the same one, or do they swap around?'

'They use whichever's free.'

'And there's no security camera covering this part of the factory?' Troy asked.

'No.'

'Who'd have access to the building after hours?'

'All my workers. I trust them entirely. They all have the access codes.'

Troy's smile was moody. 'Well, there's at least one who's south of honest.'

On their own again, Troy looked at his partner and said, 'Back to the idea of talking to them one-by-one.'

Lexi sighed. 'You'll show them a picture of Joe Catchpole and they'll all deny knowing him. But one will twitch. That's the one you'll want to arrest. But a nervous twitch is nowhere near enough.'

'I know. But that one's mobile phone will be worth checking out. Maybe there'll be tiger DNA on their overalls.' He shrugged. 'Let's come back tomorrow when they'll all be here working.'

'Unless I get any evidence overnight that needs following up.'

'It's a deal. But remember, I'm stopping up all night as well.'

'Oh yes. The attempt to run your brain down to zero.'

'Before that happens, let's look into Henry Patrick Fifteen – the doctor – and get me registered as one of his patients. Back to Shepford.'

'You're just looking for excuses to leave Pickling.'

Troy's second smile of the day was weak. 'Getting away from here's an added bonus.'

SCENE 15

Terabyte had created an artificial life for Trent Goodall. Trent was a strong sportsman, exactly the same age, weight and height as Troy. Trent's medical record was the same as Troy's, but with repeated bouts of severe insomnia. As for his career, he was a sausage-maker.

'He can't be a sausage-maker!' Lexi exclaimed. 'He doesn't have a clue what's in them.'

'That's the point,' Terabyte replied. 'Neither does anyone else. If he's asked, he can just make it up as he goes along and no one's going to argue. Fat, salt, pig, squirrel, warthog, kangaroo.'

'Very funny,' Troy muttered. Scrolling down his pseudonym's life on-screen, he yawned, turned occasionally to Terabyte and said, 'This is good.'

'Better than Troy Goodhart's life?' Lexi asked with a grin.

Bleary-eyed, Troy replied, 'Right now, almost anything would be better.'

Terabyte said, 'I consulted a medical friend about the treatments you would've had for your sleep problem.'

Troy nodded. 'North of believable.'

Terabyte accessed the surgery's database. 'Okay. I'm slipping Trent Goodall in there. You're on Dr Henry Patrick Fifteen's list of clients.' He paused before noting, 'It includes Shepford Prison. And ... '

'What? Who?'

Terabyte shook his hair away from his face. 'I'm not sure you're going to like this.'

'What?'

'Florrie Tamsin Two's one of his patients.'

Lexi groaned.

'That's bad news,' Troy said, looking at Lexi. 'Are you going to call her, or am I?'

'All right. I'll do it.'

While Lexi prepared herself, Troy said to Terabyte, 'I've got another job for you.'

'What's that?' he asked.

'Barney Woodcraft paid Nat Med for shark cartilage. His wife, Madeline, sent me the details and their bank statement. The money went to a reference number, not a name. Can you find out who really got it?'

Terabyte sucked in air. 'Tricky. The bank won't tell me, that's for sure. It's all supposed to be confidential.'

'Can't you find a back-door way of doing it?'

'Leave it with me.'

Speaking into her phone, Lexi said, 'Sorry to bother you again, Florrie. It's Lexi Four.'

The loudspeaker broadcast the biologist's reply. 'No problem. What can I do for you? Another batch of animals?'

'No. It's more personal.'

'Go on.'

Lexi took a deep breath. 'Do you have a doctor?'

'I'm registered at the local surgery. I haven't been for ages. I'm fit. Why?'

'Just a line of investigation we're following. Do you know the doctors?'

'I guess I'm assigned to one of them but I can't remember the name.'

'Henry Patrick Fifteen?'

'Could be.' She laughed. 'I think that tells you how well I know them.'

'Okay,' Lexi said. 'Thanks. I'll be in touch.'

'You're welcome.'

Troy gazed at Lexi. 'I hate to say it but her name keeps cropping up.'

Lexi pocketed her mobile. 'Coincidence,' she muttered.

'There comes a point,' said Troy, 'when a stream becomes a river, when coincidence becomes a connection. Joe Catchpole jotted her name and address down. He was treated in prison by Henry Patrick Fifteen. Now it turns out that Florrie Two's with the same doctor.'

'Look. She's written articles about endangered animals. Saving them, not killing them. One came out just the other day. She can't be involved. And she's an outer.'

'So's Henry Patrick Fifteen.'

'I'd be ashamed if any outer was dabbling in pseudo-science,' Lexi said. 'They can't possibly believe in it.'

'But they might peddle it to gullible majors.'

'Why?'

Troy shrugged. 'Because they want to get rich? I don't know.'

Terabyte interrupted. 'I'm sorry, Lexi, but I'm going to throw in another connection.'

'Which is?'

'I don't think I've got a chance of hacking this bank account – and it'd be illegal.' He glanced down at his life-logger that was recording everything to ensure fair play. 'You could apply for a warrant, I suppose, and do it properly, but I can't help noticing something about the account number.'

'What?'

'I've checked. The first eight digits are the day, month and year that Dr Henry Patrick Fifteen was born.'

Troy and Lexi looked at each other. Troy said, 'I think the coincidence theory has just been stretched beyond breaking point.'

Deflated, Lexi muttered, 'That's that, then.'

'Looks like the Woodcrafts paid Henry Patrick Fifteen. That makes him Nat Med. And his prison work gives us the link to Joe Catchpole.'

Reluctantly, Lexi updated her spreadsheet with the new information.

'I'll phone the surgery,' Troy said, 'and tell them I'm still wide awake. I need an appointment with Dr Henry Fifteen and something to help me sleep.'

SCENE 16

Troy's appointment with Dr Henry Fifteen had been arranged for Tuesday. Today, Troy and Lexi were going to interview the five butchers at Pickling squirrel farm. On the way there, Lexi nudged her partner whenever his eyelids became heavy and he verged on sleep. 'Are you sure you'll be able to spot a slight twitch that'll tell you someone's lying? Is your inbuilt lie detector still working?'

'Being tired doesn't make me useless,' Troy claimed. 'I'm not sliding to the bottom of the greasy pole yet.'

'Huh. You're not climbing up it either.'

Troy quizzed the butchers – all in clean overalls – one after the other. He soon found out that their bright blue clothing was laundered and sterilized every day. There was no point in analysing it for the DNA of animals other than squirrels. None of the butchers admitted knowing Joe Catchpole. Their reactions were suitably blank.

Knowing that Catchpole had crashed his cargo last Thursday, Troy guessed that the animal parts had been prepared on the previous evening. But, when he asked the staff for their whereabouts on Wednesday night, all five had credible alibis.

Troy believed that, despite his fatigue, he would have spotted the tell-tale signs of deceit. He saw no suspicious body language at all. Either he was more jaded than he thought, or the butchers had nothing to do with the trade in endangered animals.

Frustrated, Troy went back to the manager's office. 'Does anyone else have butchery skills on the staff?' he asked.

'I do. But you can't seriously suspect me … '

'I can seriously suspect who I like,' Troy snapped. 'What were you doing last Wednesday – evening and night-time?'

'I … er … I don't know. I'm hopeless at remembering. Let me … ' He checked his diary. 'I was out with my wife. We went to see a film.'

'Which cinema? Which movie? Tell me a bit about it.'

Lexi checked her life-logger while the manager described his night out. At the end, she nodded at Troy.

'Okay. How about this? Might one of your people have given the access codes to somebody who doesn't work here?'

'I can't rule it out, but I seriously doubt it. They wouldn't put their jobs on the line by letting a moonlighter in.'

'Have you got any sort of security at night and on Sundays?'

'Now you mention it, yes. A guard's supposed to come round every three hours. Oh,' the manager said, 'he's a butcher. Or was. He used to work here. Then he went off to see the world – touring Africa and the like. He was desperate for a job – for money – when he got back. I didn't have a vacancy for him, so he took up security instead. He walks around here and several other buildings in Pickling.' The manager smiled. 'He looks the part. Big fellah. I haven't seen him for quite a while.'

'Name?'

'David Upton.'

Troy said, 'Where does he live?'

The manager shrugged. 'In Pickling somewhere.'

'What's the name of the security company?'

'NSP. It stands for Night Security Patrol or Night Security Pickling. I can't remember.'

The detectives failed to find David Upton at NSP headquarters or at his home, but they got a description and a photo. A work colleague told them that, after each nightshift, David usually relaxed with a leisurely swim at the local sports centre before going to bed at about noon. The night patrolman was twelve hours out of sync with most majors.

It was an orderly session in the pool. The swimmers followed each other in lanes at more-or-less the same easy pace. No diving, no splashing, no messing around. Just one relentless length after another.

Troy and Lexi breathed in the distinctive chlorinated air and surveyed the bathers. 'This is the sort of swimming I did a lot of,' Lexi said, 'until this job got in the way. I was faster, though.'

When they spotted a man who matched their picture of David Upton, they went to the shallow end of his lane. Squatting, Troy waited for him as he propelled himself through the water with a lazy breast-stroke. Before he could turn, Troy shouted, 'David Upton?'

The man stopped, wiped the water from his eyes and looked puzzled. 'Yes?'

'Detective Troy Goodhart. Can I have a word?'

David glanced behind him and, before he disrupted the next swimmer, he heaved himself powerfully onto the side of the pool, water draining from his considerable frame. Standing up straight, he towered over Troy and Lexi.

Trying not to be intimidated, Troy said, 'How was Africa?'

David was bemused by the question but he answered with a grin, 'Hotter than here. Why?'

'Just checking I've got the right David Upton. The security guard who went to Africa.'

David ran a hand over his wet hair. 'That's me.'

'Shall we go somewhere more … ?'

'Good idea.' He grabbed his towel from a plastic chair and threw it around his broad shoulders.

Troy didn't want David to go to the changing room and get dressed. That would have given him a chance to escape the interview. A man wearing only swimming trunks and a towel was unlikely to run off.

Instead, Troy led the way to the rest area beside the diving pool.

They sat down on bright plastic seats and, keeping it light-hearted, Troy asked, 'Did you go on safari? Taking a look at threatened animals.'

'Yes. It was fantastic. Elephants, rhinos, lions, leopards.'

'Saiga antelope?'

'No.' David wiped his face with a corner of his towel and said, 'What's this about?'

Troy decided to drop his bombshell. 'You and Joe Catchpole.'

For a moment, David clearly wondered if he should deny all knowledge of the van driver but he realized that the split-second of hesitation had already given him away. 'Joe?'

'You know him, then?'

'Vaguely.' David paused and smiled. 'A dying breed. Driving's not a good job to have in an age of driverless cars.'

'How did you meet him?'

'I'm a security guard. He collects things from one of the firms I look after. I see him now and again and have a brief natter.'

Troy watched a procession of swimmers for a few seconds. 'Which firm?'

'The squirrel factory.'

Troy pounced. 'So, he picks goods up on Sundays or at night – when you're there but the factory's closed? That's weird.'

'Er ... Sometimes, I get there early – just before they shut up shop.'

'But the manager hasn't seen you for ages.'

David had ceased to drip water. Twisting the towel nervously around his left hand, he reddened slightly. 'I don't go inside.'

'What are these collections Joe makes?'

David looked away, suddenly taking an interest in a poolside trainer with a whistle perched between his lips. 'It's nothing to do with me.'

'Have you been in contact with him in the last few days?'

'No,' David answered.

'When did you last see him?'

Thinking, David sucked in air through his teeth. 'Erm ... I'm not sure. Sorry. I'm knackered. It's nightshift work. For me, it's nearly bedtime.'

'Yeah,' Troy replied with a sigh. 'I know how you feel but, if I can stay awake, so can you.'

David tried to change the subject. 'I know a good way to get off to sleep – if that's your problem.'

'Oh? Is it natural?'

'No, I don't think so. It's a pill. A knockout sedative.'

Troy shook his head and leaned back in the seat. Looking up at the highest diving board, he said, 'That's a long drop.'

'Ten metres,' David told him, clearly pleased to dodge further grilling.

'I've always fancied high diving,' said Lexi.

'I know,' Troy replied.

'Have I told you before?'

'No. I just know you fancy anything scary.'

Relaxed, David grinned at the young detectives.

Abruptly, Troy thrust his suspect back into the deep end. 'I repeat. When did you last see Joe Catchpole?'

'A couple of weeks back, perhaps.'

Impatient, Troy said, 'If Lexi found rhino DNA on your clothes and shoes, you'd claim it was because of your safari. Highly unlikely after all this time, but that's what you'd claim. Yes?'

'I ... er ... I suppose so.'

Troy thought that David should have been more surprised by the sudden swerve of the interview. He had probably worked out that they were investigating the illegal trade in rhino horn. Cottoning on so quickly suggested to Troy that he was a part of it. 'If she found tiger and saiga antelope DNA – and she will if you've handled either – you won't be able to blame it on your trip to Africa. Correct?'

'Yes, but … '

'You were a butcher, weren't you?'

David's attempted laugh sounded tense and false. 'Cutting up dead animals isn't as attractive as it looks.'

'Shall we go back to your house so Lexi can pull the place apart,' Troy said, 'or shall we carry on here and assume she's found the DNA? You've butchered tiger and antelope carcasses in the squirrel farm, haven't you? Lexi's already got the evidence from the factory. By my reckoning it was last Wednesday.'

David took a deep breath and stared down at his bare feet and the wet tiles. 'I haven't done anything wrong.'

Two swimmers sauntered towards the rest area. Lexi stood up, displaying her life-logger, and said, 'Police. Give us ten minutes.'

Troy fixed his gaze on David. 'Believe me, if it takes an hour, we'll take an hour. We'll start with trespass and move north from there. You went into the squirrel factory. I suppose you might say it was part of your patrol. Security business. But butchering endangered species?'

David shuffled awkwardly in his seat. 'All I did was to make them easier to dispose of.'

'That's still against the Convention on the International Trade in Endangered Species,' Lexi told him.

'I don't know … '

Irritated, Troy interrupted. 'Ignorance of the law isn't a defence against breaking it.'

David was a big man but he adopted the pose of a boy on the receiving end of a teacher's telling-off.

'Were they dead when you got your hands on them?' Troy asked.

'Er … Yes.'

Troy stared at the man who had just lied to him. 'That's not true.'

'All right. It varies. Most are dead. The bigger animals. They're in manageable pieces. Chilled. Some are anaesthetized. To keep them fresh.'

Troy was appalled. 'So you kill them.'

'Breaking CITES big time,' Lexi added.

'Does the manager – or anyone else there – know what you do?' said Troy.

'No. I need their equipment, but I put everything back afterwards. It's just me, heavy-lifting gear and Joe if I need him.'

'Who are you working for?' Troy snapped.

He shook his head. 'No idea.'

'How do you get paid?'

'After each job an envelope comes through the door. Cash.'

Lexi dived into the conversation again. 'Do you still have one of the envelopes?'

'No.'

'What about the last lot of cash?' she asked.

'Part spent, part banked.'

Troy said, 'Do you know who's behind it?'

David shook his head.

'What about Joe? Would he know?'

David looked briefly into the detective's face. 'Maybe. He was always asking questions.'

'Was?'

'I didn't mean … I just meant whenever we came together he was always more curious than was good for him.'

'In what way?'

'As I said. He asked around. He found out that there was a gang. A ruthless bunch. *Really* ruthless. I told him: it's best to do what you're told when you're dealing with people like that.'

'Where did the animals come from?'

'Northern International Airways. Before that, I don't know. When one of the baggage-handlers sees crates with a certain mark, he puts them on one side. Joe reckoned he's got no idea what he's handling. Diplomatic supplies or something. Anyway, like me, he does what he's told and takes the money. He programs a refrigerated truck – driverless – to take the crates to the squirrel farm. He calls me and Joe to let us know a shipment's on its way. I … er … prepare the body parts, then Joe takes them away for making into medicines.'

'Where?'

'All over, I think. On Wednesday, he talked about going to Shepford.'

'Who did he go to?'

Upton shrugged. 'Ask Joe. He's the nosy one.'

'What's the name of the baggage-handler?'

'I don't know. He just calls himself V.'

Troy said, 'Did you meet anyone in the black-market trade when you were in Africa?'

Again, he bowed his head. 'Not that I'm aware of. The guide told me about it. That's all. They tell anyone who'll listen.'

Troy looked towards his partner and she nodded at him. 'Okay,' said Troy. 'Lexi's going to call in some uniformed officers. You're going to be arrested under suspicion of offences against the Convention on the International Trade in Endangered Species. We'll have more questions later.'

While local officers walked away with David Upton, Lexi said, 'Considering you're feeling lousy, that was quite a performance. You skewered him. Like an angry rhino.'

'I'm beginning to feel like an angry rhino.'

'I did warn you.'

'Sometimes it pays to get stroppy.' Troy yawned. 'This is a big machine we're trying to crack. We know a couple of cogs, but what about the engine? Stop that and it doesn't go anywhere. But we're a long way off.'

'Let's go to the airport. They've got loads of security cameras. Hey presto. We'll get V, the baggage-handler.'

Troy shrugged, unimpressed. Doing anything required such a lot of effort and his reserves were very low. 'Another small cog.'

'Better than nothing.'

'All right.'

SCENE 17

Monday 19th May, Early evening

The security staff at Northern International Airways had set up a small private room for Lexi and Troy. There, the detectives had spent the afternoon examining closed-circuit TV footage of the goods coming off aircraft on Wednesday. Troy had tried to play his part, but his concentration had drifted and he'd dozed off regularly. Lexi had done most of the work and she was the one who'd found what they were looking for.

Together, they showed the sequence to a baggage-handler called Victor Newsome.

'No one takes any notice,' Troy said. 'You're just doing your job. Lifting crates and boxes into waiting trucks. But when this flight comes in from China, you put all the cargo into the truck down here on the left.' Troy pointed with his finger on the screen. 'Except for four crates that you take off and put on their own in a different truck. Why do they get special treatment?'

'Erm … '

Interrupting immediately, Troy said, 'We've spoken to David Upton and Joe Catchpole. And we've checked the truck's programming. You sent it to Pickling squirrel factory – without a passenger. That's a traffic offence. So think about it. Lying to throw us off the scent is another crime.'

'I'm just following instructions.'

'Whose instructions?'

'As far as I know, the airport's. Some cases go to different places.' Victor shrugged. 'What's wrong with that?'

'You're known as V, aren't you?'

'Am I?'

Troy banged the table with his fist. 'Come on!'

For an instant, Victor looked into Troy's face and Troy realized that this man was far more frightened of someone else than he was of a short-tempered detective. It didn't matter what Troy said or did.

Victor Newsome was not going to reveal anything significant. He would rather go to prison than face the fury of a heartless gangland boss.

For a moment, Troy wondered whether he should leave Victor and David in place. He considered offering them a sympathetic hearing of their crimes in return for carrying on and informing him of developments. That way, he and Lexi could shadow the next batch of incoming animals and monitor everyone involved from airport touchdown to end use. But he decided not to bother. Some gangster had terrified the two men so much that he would never be able to tame them.

'What was in the crates?'

Victor shrugged again. 'I shift hundreds every day. I don't have time to look. I don't worry about it.'

'Dead animals. Some drugged ones.'

'If you say so.'

'Endangered animals. Doesn't that bother you?'

'It's not my fault.'

Troy sighed. 'One last time. Who pays you? Who stuffs the cash into your envelope?'

Victor shook his head. 'One last time. I don't know what you're talking about.'

'I was right,' Troy muttered to himself. 'A very small cog.'

'I'll arrange the arrest,' said Lexi.

'Okay,' Troy replied. Glancing at Victor, he added, 'Maybe you'll feel safe in a police cell. Safe enough to talk.'

Victor grunted. 'You're dafter than you look if you think I'm safe anywhere.'

SCENE 18

After midnight, The Hungry Human was used to serving only outer food. There was very little call for the major menu but, for a sleepless Troy, the café produced toad-in-the-hole, swamped with brown sauce.

Lexi grimaced. 'Toad. So, that's what's in sausages.'

Not in the mood for teasing, Troy muttered, 'No shepherds in shepherd's pie, no toad in this. As you know. It's just a name.'

'Do you realize,' Lexi said, 'that we've barely been

apart for sixty-four hours? Three days, two nights. Soon be three nights.'

'Weird.'

'Amazing we haven't murdered each other.'

'Plenty of time before I go to the doctor.' Troy's shoulders were drooping and the bags under his eyes were pronounced. His legs felt like lead weights.

'I'll help you get into your role. Test you on the life and times of Trent Goodall.'

'Thanks.'

'I'll meditate after this,' she said, waving a hand at her bowl of yellow-jacket wasp larvae, 'and then we'll do it.'

'I was thinking …' Troy's attention seemed to slip.

'About?'

He rubbed both eyes. 'Slaughtering things. I guess we kill more animals than they kill us, but which creature kills most human beings? Sharks? Bears? I don't know.'

Lexi laughed. 'Nowhere near close. Dogs, snakes and hippos kill loads more, with tsetse flies way ahead. But two are in an entirely different league. Neck and neck, the big killers are mosquitos and …'

Troy waited, too tired to play games.

' … human beings.'

Troy nodded. 'That figures. Malaria and wars.'

'Yeah. Bites and bombs.'

Suddenly switching back to the case, Troy said, 'By taking two little cogs out of the machine, we're sending a message to whoever's in charge. Whether we want to or not.'

'I know. If they're as brutal as we think, we're making ourselves targets. You'd better be careful – especially in *your* state.'

For once, Lexi's house was not buzzing with her outer friends. There was only one friend. Her partner in crime: Detective Troy Goodhart. A major.

For Lexi, coming out of meditation was like surfacing from a still lake. It was a return to the choppy, imperfect world after total immersion in tranquillity. Calm replaced by chaos. Troy was dozing in an armchair instead of immersing himself in the life of his alter ego, Trent Goodall.

'Hey!' Lexi called out.

Troy jolted. 'Just resting my eyes,' he murmured.

'So, you'll be perfect when I quiz you about Trent Goodall.'

'It'll be the first time I get a hundred per cent in an exam.'

Troy was faultless on when and where Trent was born, his childhood diseases, his schooling, his recent move to Shepford and registering at Dr Henry Patrick Fifteen's clinic. He was not so good on Trent's therapies for sleeplessness. He got four questions wrong.

Lexi shook her head at him. 'I said you'd better be careful. You haven't even learnt your lines.'

Troy was unconcerned. 'It doesn't matter. He's not going to ask me any of these things. Anyway, no one's perfect. It'd be fishy if I could tell him every treatment, every pill and the date of every appointment.'

'Well … okay. I guess you've got a point,' Lexi admitted.

'I'll be fine. Don't worry.'

Lexi had never worried about a major before, but she was concerned for this one. She glanced at her life-logger. 'Seven hours to go before you're due at the surgery. Want to go through it again, or indulge in some outer nightlife?'

Troy managed a smile. 'I know which is more likely to keep me awake.'

SCENE 19

Troy was no longer a police officer. He was a sausage-maker. He was no longer Troy Goodhart. He was Trent Goodall. He was not wearing a detective's life-logger, only a concealed microphone. But he was suffering from the effects of a sleep disorder.

The large screen in the waiting room of the surgery bleeped and a message appeared. Trent Goodall would be seen now by Dr Henry Patrick Fifteen in Room 5.

The doctor was smartly dressed. White coat, red tie and brown trousers. He was about thirty years of age with thinning fair hair. Eyes fixed on his monitor, probably scanning Trent's medical record, he barely looked up at his patient. Waving towards the chair, he said, 'Take a seat.' Finally, he made eye contact with Trent Goodall. 'Right. Hello. I'm duty-bound to ask you a question first. Would you prefer to see a major doctor?'

Taken by surprise, Trent said, 'Do you have one?'

Henry Fifteen smiled. 'They are rather thin on the ground. You can opt for ours but there'd be a sizeable wait. We have major nurses, though.'

Trent shrugged. 'It doesn't matter. I know you don't sleep, but I'm sure you can help someone who does – or should, but can't.'

'Is that the problem?' The doctor glanced at his screen once more before adding, 'Again.'

'Yes.'

Henry Fifteen nodded and gazed into his patient's face. 'I can see that you're under the weather. Tell me your symptoms.'

'I haven't slept for the last three days. I'm shattered. Everything aches. My legs, arms and head. Especially my legs. I doze a bit, but proper sleep … No. My friends and family tell me I'm stroppy and not really with it half the time.'

The doctor nodded. 'But none of the usual

sedatives have helped you in the past. Not in the long term.'

'No.'

'You've exhausted every obvious medication. But there are other options. I could refer you to a sleep disorder clinic for psychological and specialist medical assessment, for instance. I'm surprised your previous doctor didn't recommend it. Anyway, tell me a bit more about you. That may help us find a way forward. I see you're a sausage-maker.' With a forced grin, he asked, 'What on earth are they made of?'

'Toads.'

'Toads?'

'Not really. It's what an outer friend thinks – because of toad-in-the-hole.'

'Very droll. Would you describe it as a high-pressure job?'

'No.'

'When you get into bed at night, are you thinking about your work or do you have other things on your mind?'

'I'm too tired to have anything on my mind – except dropping off.'

'Perhaps you're trying too hard to sleep. It happens.'

'I just need a little help.'

'If you like, I can make an enquiry about an appointment at the sleep clinic. In the meantime, there's another avenue.'

'Oh?'

'Natural medicine.'

'I've heard about that,' Trent said.

Henry Fifteen glanced at his new patient. 'Where?'

'Online.'

'Ah. Everyone's favourite source of medical advice. What specifically have you heard?'

'People talk about powdered tiger claws.'

'Yes. Unconventional, but it's used.'

'Would you take it if you were in my position?'

'That's difficult to say, because I can't suffer like you. But I understand that desperate situations can lead to desperate measures. You see, when you take medication, one of three things can happen. It could help you, it could do nothing at all or, because you believe it will work, it might make you feel better – even though it's doing nothing at all.'

Trent yawned. 'Are you saying it's worth a try?'

'Yes, but there's a snag.'

'What's that?'

'It's expensive. Very expensive.'

'Oh. I didn't have to pay for any of the other pills.'

Dr Henry Fifteen replied, 'This is from a different, private source.'

'Desperate situations call for desperate measures.'

'I don't know how much a sausage-maker earns.'

'Not enough, probably. But I have helpful parents.'

The doctor smiled. 'I guess families have their uses.'

'Who would I have to pay?'

'Me.'

'So, you have this medicine?'

'Once you complete payment, it'll be here the following morning. You can drop by to pick it up.'

'Sounds good. Do you prepare it yourself?'

'Why do you ask?'

Trent shrugged. 'It's just that, if I know it's something you've made, I'll have more faith in it.'

Henry Fifteen nodded. 'All right. The more belief you have, the more likely it is to work. I'll formulate it myself.'

'Thanks.'

The doctor scribbled his bank details on a piece of paper and handed it to Trent. 'That is what you'll need to make the payment.'

Trent glanced down at the account code and saw a familiar number.

They negotiated a price and Trent Goodall

promised to arrange a transfer of money after lunch.

'Then it will be available to collect from reception in the morning,' Henry Fifteen told him. 'And, by the way, don't worry about what it says on the outside of the packaging. Inside, it will be exactly what you want.'

With a groan, Trent got to his feet wearily. 'Okay. Thanks.'

Outside, well away from the surgery, Trent turned back into Troy Goodhart. Lexi said, 'I bet you were tempted to arrest him there and then.'

'I thought of Quang Xuan's tigers that turned out to be cats. Let's get the stuff and analyse it first.'

'Agreed.'

'Terabyte will have to sort out payment from a fictional account. In the name of Mr and Mrs Goodall.'

'He's already working on it,' said Lexi. 'And I've already requested a huge amount of money from the commander, promising we'll get it back afterwards.'

'Good.'

'What's next?'

'Sleep,' Troy replied bluntly.

SCENE 20

Wednesday 21st May, Early morning

Lexi rang the bell and then waited. She was cool. Her heart rate was normal. But she hoped that Troy would come to the door rather than his grandmother. Lexi knew that Troy's grandma did not mix well with outers. Lexi also knew that his gran's son – Troy's father – had died twelve days ago and that, for majors, there was no greater hurt than the loss of their flesh and blood. Perhaps Lexi was a little nervy.

The person who opened the door wasn't the hardened woman Lexi had expected. Mrs

Goodhart was elderly and rather worn. Maybe that was the effect of recent events. 'Yes?' she prompted.

'Sorry to bother you,' Lexi said, 'but my name's Lexi Iona Four. I'm Troy's partner.'

'Yes?'

'Is Troy in – and out of bed yet?'

'He's tired out. It's because of you working all hours that he's under pressure to do the same. He can't. He's a major. He needs his sleep.'

'I know, but … ' Lexi hesitated, wondering whether to defend herself or not. 'It was something he wanted to do. I told him not to.'

'Really?'

Still standing outside, Lexi said, 'Yes.'

Troy's grandma sighed. 'I suppose you'd better come in.'

'Thanks, Gr … ' Lexi stopped herself and smiled. 'Oops. I was about to call you Gran. That would've been … '

'Wrong.'

'Yes.'

Troy came into the hallway with an expression of surprise. And concern. 'Oh. Are you two getting on all right?'

Gran grunted and walked away.

Relieved, Lexi said, 'Hey. You look almost human again.'

'Come in.' Troy paused and whispered, 'Have we paid yet? Am I the lucky owner of some crunched up claws?'

'That's what I came to tell you. It's all done. You can collect them any time. The surgery opened ten minutes ago.'

'You could've sent a message.'

'I was … I wanted to check you were okay.'

Troy grinned. 'You can't wait to get your hands on the powder. A message wouldn't wake me up, but a knock on the door would.'

'Maybe that as well. I've got a sequencer on standby.'

'*And* you wondered what my place was like.'

'Huh. You can stop using your mind-reading tricks on me now. Keep it for the suspects.' She walked over to a sideboard. Pointing to a photo perched on top, she asked, 'Is this your mum and dad?'

'Just before I was born.'

'Strange,' Lexi said.

'What is?'

'Knowing whose eggs and sperm went into making you. Even having a picture.'

Feeling fresher than he had for several days, Troy smiled. 'Do you have a picture of an incubator?'

Gran brought in two glasses of blueberry juice on an old-fashioned tray. She glanced at Lexi and said, 'We don't have your sort of drink. No beer. None of your food, either.' She shivered at the thought.

Pleased and surprised that politeness had trumped prejudice, Lexi said, 'That's fine. Thank you.'

Troy nodded appreciatively at his grandmother.

After she left, Lexi moved the juice to one side. 'How's she coping, your grandmother?'

'On the surface, she's okay. But underneath … Something's bubbling like lava. One day, there'll be an eruption. All the hurt about Dad will come out in a massive explosion. Or something like that.'

Lexi nodded but, as an outer, she didn't really understand. She turned her attention back to the case. 'Did you notice Henry Patrick Fifteen's account number?'

'I could hardly keep my eyes open but, yes, I saw.'

'It's the same reference number that Barney and Madeline Woodcraft paid.'

'Meaning he's Nat Med.'

'Yes. We definitely need to analyse what he's selling.'

'What have you been doing while I've caught up a bit on sleep?'

'Looking for Joe Catchpole, finding nothing. Going through files in case somebody reported something unusual to the police last Thursday. Nothing yet. Checking up on registration numbers of the cars that slowed down to get a good look at the crashed van. That uniformed policeman had them on his life-logger.'

'And?'

'I've got a list of owners, but my spreadsheet hasn't flagged anything up. No criminal records, no one working with animals or in medicine, no one with known connections to any suspect.'

Troy finished his own juice and then quickly downed Lexi's as well. That way, his grandma would think that their outer visitor had made an effort to fit in. 'But,' he said, 'you've got more people who knew where the crash happened.'

Lexi nodded. 'The ones who drove past, Florrie, Susannah Appleyard, Catchpole and us – the police and forensic scientists. One of them told the gang so they could hijack the van.'

'That policeman. Was he just the nearest available cop, or did he volunteer to guard the crime scene?'

'I don't know. But I'll find out.'

Troy stood up. 'Let's go to the clinic and collect my medicine.'

SCENE 21

Wednesday 21st May, Afternoon

In Shepford Crime Central, Troy and Lexi were waiting to find out what was in Dr Henry Patrick Fifteen's cure for insomnia. But they weren't just waiting.

Lexi looked up from her laptop and said, 'That uniformed cop. The one stationed at the crash site. According to his boss, he volunteered for the job.'

'I don't want to point the finger at one of our own,' Troy replied, 'but did you see him make any calls or send any messages?'

'No. Did you?'

'No.'

'He was there before us,' said Lexi. 'If he contacted anyone, it could've been before we arrived.'

'You'd better put him on the list of possible informants.'

She smiled. 'I already have.'

'How long's it going to take before we get an answer on the tiger claws?'

'A few hours yet. Sometime tonight, just before or just after midnight. Are you going to stop up again, or are you back to normal? At least, as normal as a major gets.'

'It's important. I'm in for the duration.'

'Well, make sure your grandmother doesn't blame me.' She turned her attention back to her laptop and, within minutes, said, 'Hey. Here's something.'

'What?'

'It might have nothing to do with us, but somebody living near Shepford Crematorium called the police last Thursday night. They noticed activity. To quote the report, puffs of smoke.'

'So?'

'According to this neighbour, the crematorium was closed for redecoration at the time.'

Troy hesitated. 'Did anyone follow it up?'

'No. Low priority. Maybe whoever took the call

thought it was imagination – or kids mucking about.'

Troy nodded. 'It was the day Joe Catchpole disappeared.'

'Yeah. Someone might've wanted to get rid of a body that night.'

'We know our gang borrows Pickling squirrel farm when it's closed. Maybe it borrows the crematorium as well.'

Lexi glanced at the clock on her laptop. 'Plenty of time before we get the results.'

'All right. Let's go and have a chat with the witness.'

SCENE 22

Ollie was too old to be employed. From the position of the worn chair in his living room, Troy could tell that the retired major spent a long time gazing out of the window, taking in the restful view of fields, a wood to the left and the crematorium slightly to the right.

'Nice scenery,' Troy said to him.

'Lovely. You can see I overlook the crematorium.'

'Does it smell?'

'No. There's an afterburner. I asked one of the men who work there. It gets rid of smell and smoke. All you get is the odd puff of smoke – when they first start up the burners. It's not much.'

'Is that what you saw on Thursday?'

'No. There was more than usual. And there was something of a smell. That's not normal at all. It was like they hadn't got the afterburner working properly.'

To Troy, Ollie seemed to be a kindly busybody with too much time on his hands and too little to do. That was what Troy hoped to exploit. 'When you saw it – and smelled it – did you keep an eye on the place for a while?'

'For a good while, yes. I was puzzled. They told me it was shut for at least a week while they were decorating the entrance and main hall.' Just for a moment, he looked wistful. 'I've been in it to see off a few friends and family. I can tell you, it needed a lick of paint.'

After death, many majors were buried in the grounds of temples, but some requested cremation. Almost all outers were cremated. It was done without fuss and with little ceremony. After all, it was only a matter of disposing of waste safely.

'Thursday evening. Wasn't it dark?'

'That's a good question,' Ollie said, apparently admiring Troy's ability to probe the incident. 'It was a bright moon, almost full, and a clear sky. A nice night. That's why I could see the smoke. There's no doubt in my mind. None.'

Troy gazed across the field and into the car park. Right now, there were two red vans outside the building. Workers were replacing the large front windows. 'Were there any cars? Would it have been light enough to see? Even if it was too dark, you would've spotted any cars coming and going.'

'Now that's another good one. I can see why they made you a detective, young man. No. There weren't any cars.'

'It's quite a long walk from the main road,' Troy said, glancing at his partner.

'Quite right,' Ollie replied. 'You wouldn't want to carry … anything heavy all that way.'

In Troy's mind, the obvious and awful conclusion was simple. If someone had been reduced to ash last Thursday, that person must have walked to the crematorium.

SCENE 23

Wednesday 21st May, Early evening

The engineers had finished fitting new frames and windows in the crematorium entrance. When Troy and Lexi arrived, they were completing the job by clearing up the mess that they'd made. They told the detectives they'd had to go inside the building, but the only part they'd entered was the reception. They had not gone anywhere near the furnaces.

The entrance and main hall were sunlit and airy, deliberately suggesting brightness. The space and facilities were used mostly by outers, so there were no religious symbols. It was designed for celebrating each life once it had come to an end.

The character of the crematorium changed as Troy and Lexi went down the corridor marked *Staff Only*. Here, the appearance and atmosphere became more business-like. It was functional. A job had to be done and it had to be done well. On the left was a room where bodies were prepared. Majors and some outers opted to remain within sealed coffins. Many outers were taken from their wooden caskets, wrapped and placed in strong cardboard boxes, allowing the coffins to be reused. Outers were not sentimental about the treatment of their remains, and it seemed a waste to burn perfectly good wooden caskets. By the door there was a gurney, ready to take each prepared corpse to the furnace.

'This is where it gets interesting,' Lexi said, scanning ahead. 'Let me go first. I'm looking for signs of a struggle – or anything else. Prints, hair, fibres.'

Troy nodded. 'I guess there's only a couple of workers who come down here. Eliminate them and everything else might be significant.'

'Not quite,' Lexi said as she approached the final room with a grim smile. 'An awful lot of dead people come this way.' She slipped into a nylon overall from her forensic kit bag and gave latex gloves and shoe covers to Troy. She pulled on her own gloves and then she opened the door.

The cremation chamber was not large. Opposite Lexi and Troy stood a row of three integrated furnaces. Each of them had a sturdy door – like a domestic oven but large enough to take a coffin. Right now, all three doors were closed. Above each one was a black sooty stain.

'I'll stay back,' Troy said.

'This makes you queasy.' Lexi's comment was almost a question.

'I just don't want to contaminate the room.'

Lexi grinned. 'Sure.' As she walked to the far side of the furnaces, she said, 'It's clean. Pretty much spotless. Good. If anyone's been in here since it was cleaned, I'll find something.' She examined the control panel attached to the side wall of the ovens. 'Yeah. I reckon I could operate this. It's not rocket science.' She pressed the button that opened the middle furnace and the shutter rose up slowly and smoothly. Inside, there was a metal frame and rollers. It was exactly the same height off the ground as the gurney. A body could be wheeled right up to it and easily pushed into the oven on the rollers. Underneath the space where a body would lie were powerful burners. The afterburner was positioned above it.

Near Lexi, a long metallic rake was propped against the wall. She looked carefully at the handle without touching. 'It's for smashing the bigger bits of dried bone left after cremation and scraping the remains into the tray behind the shutter,' she said, almost to herself. 'I might be able to find prints or skin flakes on it. Fireproof gloves over there. I'll take those back to the lab as well. There'll be DNA inside.'

Dangling from a hook, there was a pair of tongs for handling hot trays of ashes. 'Worth checking,' Lexi muttered. At her feet, six empty metal trays lay on the floor. 'That's where the ashes are left to cool,' she said. 'I don't think I'll get anything from them.'

Gazing across the chamber, she saw a grinder in the furthest corner. 'That's for crumbling what's left.' She glanced at her partner and said, 'What we all call ashes aren't ashes, of course. Not really. It's dried and broken-up bone. But it's a grey powder after going through the blender, so it looks like ashes.' Turning her attention back to the furnaces, she opened the two remaining doors and peered inside the ovens. Both were free of calcified bone and ash. 'No obvious signs of a body,' she said. She was about to turn away from the unit on the left when she hesitated. 'Just a second.' She reached in as far as she could and scrabbled around with her fingertips, trying to grasp something that she'd seen glinting. Once she had it securely between her gloved forefinger and thumb, she extracted it from the furnace.

'What is it?' asked Troy.

She held it up to the light. 'Hard to tell. It's partly melted brass. I think... Yeah, it's a stud – from a pair of jeans. I'd be very surprised if the professionals ever burnt a body in jeans with metal studs.' She sealed it in an evidence bag. 'Someone sloppy – or somebody in a hurry – did this.'

'I think I'll go out and get some fresh air while you finish off.'

'Okay,' Lexi said, knowing the visit would not be easy for her partner. 'I'll be here a while. I'm going to take a lot of samples. I want every scrap.'

'You're going to be methodical.'

'It's the only way.'

Outside, the red vans and engineers had gone. Troy stood still, removed his gloves and slip-ons, and breathed deeply three times. Away from the inner chamber, the whole place was deliberately tranquil.

Troy's father had not been cremated. He had been buried in the temple's cemetery. Even so, Troy's mind went back to his dad's funeral and stirred up all sorts of disturbing memories. Troy plonked himself down on a bench, shut his eyes and put his head in his hands.

In a way, he wished he was more like Lexi. She accepted that one day, like everyone else, she would die, possibly at the hands of a ruthless criminal. And, when it happened, there'd be no regrets. There would simply be an end. There would be ashes blown away by the wind. Troy wished that he could also accept that death was an inevitable consequence of life. He wished that he had no regrets over his father's death.

His only advantage over Lexi was his faith. He did not believe there would be a simple and sudden end. Some part of his father had drifted away on an unearthly breeze and come to rest in a better place. There, in heaven, Troy's mother and father were together, waiting.

When Troy opened his eyes again, he saw a small round piece of metal lurking in the lawn, about a metre away from his right foot. It was just like the piece that Lexi had plucked from the furnace. He didn't move towards it. Rather, he lifted his shoes so he did not leave any further impressions on the grassy earth. If someone had destroyed a body inside and thrown the remains away here on the lawn, Troy was sitting in a crime scene, contaminating the evidence.

He cast his eyes around the ground. And he spotted another partially melted brass stud. Also, was the area tainted with grey? Possibly. He wasn't sure. It could be the shadow of a cloud or it could be his imagination.

With an unsettling feeling of horror, he could see how a gang might have marched their victim along the track and into the deserted crematorium. Like a temple, it would not be locked, so that mourners could come and go at any time, leaving tributes at the site where their loved ones had departed. The gang could have simply walked in. Perhaps they had tormented the victim with threats of incineration to extract information. Perhaps it was straightforward punishment. The ultimate punishment. Either way, Troy hoped that the victim had not been conscious when bundled into the furnace. After the flames had done their job, the gang would have gathered up the ashes, crumbled the calcified remains and discarded the lot heartlessly right here – like meaningless trash.

Rather than walking back across the area to return to the building, Troy sent Lexi a message. *When you've finished in there, you've got work to do out here. More studs, possibly more ash.*

SCENE 24

A small team of forensic scientists set about analysing all of the samples that Lexi had salvaged from the crematorium, from the microscopic particles of skin to the tongs, rake and fireproof gloves.

Lexi soon reported the first rough result. She looked across at Troy and said, 'I collected a couple of fibres. To be confirmed by chemical analysis, but they match the denim fibres from the driver's seat of Catchpole's van.'

Troy nodded. 'Meaning he was wearing jeans? Ones that may have been held together with studs?'

'Yes.'

'It's not looking good for Joe Catchpole.'

'Or for us. I wanted you to ask him why he wrote down Florrie's name and address.'

'Me too.'

Lexi looked down at her life-logger. 'It's come in. What you've been waiting for. We've got a result on your powdered claws. The DNA belongs to a Siberian tiger.'

At once, Troy jumped up. 'That fits, then. Let's go get Dr Henry Patrick Fifteen.'

Lexi smiled. 'It'll be a pleasure.'

Looking smug, Henry Patrick Fifteen announced, 'Queen captures knight,' and popped a few fried caterpillars into his mouth.

Ten small tables were laid out in the hall and at each of them sat one player. The opponents could be anywhere in the world. They were present in the hall only as images on monitors placed on the other side of each chessboard.

The chess-playing doctor looked up from his looming triumph and saw one of his recent patients approaching. Still smooth, but less self-satisfied, he said, 'You're looking better. My prescription has had an almost immediate effect.' He smiled cynically.

'I take it that you aren't all you seemed to be.'

'I'm not Trent Goodall, no. I'm Detective Troy Goodhart. And this is Detective Lexi Iona Four. You, though. You're Nat Med and we're arresting you on suspicion of offences against the Convention on the International Trade in Endangered Species.' He paused and then added, 'Detective captures crook.'

'Very droll. But you can wait, surely. I'm going to win this match in three moves.'

Troy shook his head. 'I don't think so. You're coming with us. Now.' Into the microphone he said to the opponent, 'He's thrown in the towel. It's your game.'

SCENE 25

Thursday 22nd May, Morning

Refreshed by sleep, Troy interviewed Henry Patrick Fifteen in the morning. He hoped that a restless night in an uncomfortable police cell had softened up the doctor.

Troy slid a piece of paper across the table in Shepford Crime Central and tapped it near the writing. 'Is that your bank account code? It starts with your birth date.'

'You know it is.'

'I also know it's Nat Med's account, so are you admitting you're Nat Med, supplier of natural remedies?'

'That's the logical deduction.'

'You sold me tiger claws and Barney Woodcraft bought shark cartilage from you.'

The doctor shrugged.

'If you had cancer,' Troy asked, 'would you tackle it with shark cartilage?'

'No comment.'

Lexi's temperament was set permanently to calm, but this time she could not contain her anger. 'As an outer, I'm ashamed of you,' she said. 'Dabbling in pseudo-science and trading in threatened animals. Not to mention selling stuff that doesn't work to vulnerable people.'

'No comment.'

Troy took control again. 'You expected a shipment from Joe Catchpole last Thursday, didn't you?'

'Yes.'

'It turned up late, I imagine.'

'No comment.'

'There was an accident,' Troy told him, 'and Catchpole went missing.'

'Oh, dear.'

'Can you shed any light on that?'

'If he's disappeared, he'll have been punished. I doubt very much if you'll find him alive.'

'Who will have punished him?'

'No comment.'

'Who?' Troy repeated.

'You have no idea what you're getting into,' said Henry Fifteen. 'None at all.'

'Tell me.'

'The person you want is utterly unfeeling. She'd kill someone like Catchpole with no more thought than she gives to tigers.'

'*She*?'

The doctor shuffled in his seat. 'I'm not saying any more.'

Troy gazed into the doctor's face. The bravado and arrogance had gone. After his slip, he was genuinely terrified. If it turned out that incineration was the gang's regular punishment, Troy could understand the fear. 'When were you last in contact with Florrie Tamsin Two?' he said.

'Who?'

'Are you saying you don't know her?'

Henry Patrick Fifteen hesitated and folded his arms defensively across his chest. 'No comment.'

Plainly, a restless night in an uncomfortable police cell had not softened him up that much. But his body language and his refusal to answer told its own story. Troy said, 'She's one of your patients.'

'Is she? I don't recall seeing her.'

Changing the direction of the verbal tussle, Troy asked, 'Where's Thursday's shipment? Have you got it?'

'I presume you'll search my house and surgery?'

'Of course.'

'Then, yes, you'll find the new batch of material.'

'When did you get it?'

'In the early hours of Friday.'

'Who delivered it?'

'No comment.'

'What about the van itself? Do you have it?'

'No. It's been destroyed. Along with a pick-up truck.'

'What's your role in all this? You receive animal parts, turn them into natural medicines and sell them,' said Troy. 'What else?'

'I think you have spelled it out adequately. I don't do anything else.'

'What do you do with the money you take off people like Barney Woodcraft?'

Refusing to answer, he shook his head.

'If you keep it,' said Troy, taunting him, 'that'd make you the boss. Then you'd be in for a lot more charges.'

'All right. I siphon a little. The rest goes automatically to another account. I don't know whose. It's just a number.'

'How much contact do you have with the rest of the operation?'

'None.'

'But you know there's a woman at its heart.'

'No comment.'

'Major or outer?'

'No comment.'

'Is Joe Catchpole the only one, or are other people delivering animals from other countries?'

'You're asking the wrong person,' Henry Fifteen answered. 'I am not the boss. I don't know.'

'Does he only deliver to you or are there other people like you?'

'I am not the only one.'

Lexi could not contain another outburst. 'Why are you doing it?'

'Because if I didn't, someone else would and I would be punished.'

Lexi shook her head. 'That's a rubbish excuse.'

'Look,' he replied. 'You're wrong about selling stuff that doesn't work, as you so elegantly phrased it. For those who believe in it, natural medicine works and it works well. They get a lot of relief. It's the placebo effect and it's scientifically proven.'

'Yes, it can make them feel better because they think they're getting something really powerful,' Lexi replied, 'but it doesn't cure anything. Tiger claws won't fix insomnia and bits of a shark won't cure cancer.'

'No comment.'

Troy said, 'Whether it works or not, we're going to charge you with crimes against CITES and, unless you start naming names, with obstructing our enquiries as well.'

'No comment.'

'We can arrange a new identity and a safe place to go.'

'No, you cannot.'

Troy put his head on one side for a few seconds. 'Are you trying to tell me the gang's got someone connected to the police force? A mole who leaks information.'

'No comment.'

Troy thought for a moment. 'Here's an idea. If there's a bad apple in our cart, I've got a way of finding out who it is.'

Henry Fifteen smirked as if not interested.

'We'll put it about that you've talked, so we're moving you to a safe house. Here's the trick. We leak different addresses to different people. Then we set up surveillance at each address to see what happens and who turns up. The place the gang raids gives us the mole.'

Henry Fifteen looked horrified, just as Troy intended. 'You can't do that.'

'Why not?'

'If word got out – if … anyone thought I'd talked to the police – you'd make me a target for the rest of my life.'

Troy said, 'You'll be wrapped up nice and secure in a police cell. A new ID will take care of the future.'

Henry Fifteen shook his head. 'You have a duty to look after witnesses and suspects.'

'Humans have a duty to look after animals,' Lexi muttered.

'The thing is,' Troy continued, 'you might as well tell us all you know because we're going to tell everyone you already have. If you talk, we won't have to broadcast it. You've got nothing to lose.'

Henry put his head in his hands and groaned.

'We'll leave you to have a think about it for a while.'

Lexi downed the last of her ice-cold cider in one long swig from a large jug. 'For a major, that was a clever plan. Why don't we just do it? Plant the idea that he's squealed.'

'Because, if he's burnt alive at some point in the future, I don't want it on my conscience. I don't want him punished because I pretended he'd blabbed about the boss.'

'He deserves it.'

'He's right. We have a duty of care … '

'I know.' Lexi let out a long sigh. 'Interesting that he dropped a violent "she" into the conversation, though.' She hesitated before adding, 'At least he hasn't had anything to do with Florrie Two.'

'Hasn't he?' Troy popped two pieces of mint chocolate into his mouth.

Lexi gazed at her partner. 'When you said her name, he went, "Who?" '

'And when I asked if he knows her, he refused to answer.'

'That doesn't mean … '

'I know.' Troy juggled the chocolate in his mouth. 'A shaky "No comment" isn't going to convince me one way or the other. But, if it's got nothing to do with Florrie Two, why didn't he just say so?'

Lexi shrugged. 'Do you think he's stewed long enough?'

'No. I haven't finished this chocolate yet.'

Dr Henry Patrick Fifteen didn't have sweat rolling down his face, but Troy recognized small signs of pressure. He looked gaunt and fidgeted with his hands. 'Do I have a cast-iron guarantee of a new identity in a place I choose?'

'I can get the commander to come and agree to it, if you like. But I think you might want to listen to our experts on where. Some places would be ... unwise.'

'A different country?'

'I'd have to check, but I'm sure it could be arranged.'

'And all-round protection?'

'If you agree to testify, yes.'

Henry paused. When he looked up at both detectives sitting opposite him, he said, 'You two are dicing with death. Get in her way – or in the way of her business – and ... '

'Are you threatening us?' said Troy.

'No. You should have noticed that I'm not in a position to do that. I am trying to be helpful. I'm warning you. Alerting you to danger.' He smiled cynically. 'When you know what she's like, I guarantee that you *will* lose sleep. You won't dare to shut your eyes.'

'Who is she?'

'You already know, it seems. You mentioned her. Florrie Tamsin Two.'

Ignoring the intake of breath from his partner, Troy

asked, 'Are you confirming that Florrie Tamsin Two is behind the trade in endangered animals?'

'Yes. I've never even met her. I wouldn't know what she looks like, but I know it's her.'

'How?'

'You know what happens. Names get mentioned.'

'By?'

'Joe Catchpole for one.'

Troy nodded. 'What did he say about her?'

'Mr Catchpole was talkative, to put it mildly. He talked about anything and everyone. He asked about everything and anyone. Whilst unloading, he would tell me things, including several things that I didn't really want to know. He found out about Florrie Two and listed her many acts of cruelty.'

'Such as?'

'How a fire destroyed the home and family of an importer who no longer wished to be a part of her operation. It was made to look like an accident. How a client drowned after threatening to go to the authorities because rhino horn was ineffective. That was not an accident either.'

'These could be folk tales,' Troy said. 'Passed around to scare everyone into behaving.'

'Not in Joe Catchpole's opinion.'

'Do you have dates, names?'

'No.'

'You know how the law works. Gossip doesn't count. Do you have anything solid? Proof – or things you've seen or heard yourself?'

Henry Fifteen shrugged. 'I have said all I'm going to say.'

'It's helpful, but not enough for a conviction.'

'With respect, that's your problem, not mine.'

'Florrie Tamsin Two,' Troy mumbled to himself in the corridor outside the interview room. 'Weird, but it fits.'

'Does it?'

'She knows the animals and the trade well enough. She's not short of cash. You saw her car and clothes. She knew where the van crashed so she could organize the hijack. And she knew where to look for Joe Catchpole.'

'But it doesn't make sense,' Lexi protested. 'She wouldn't.'

'You like her, I know, but she's still top of the list.'

'Huh. You believe in instinct, don't you? I'm telling you she wouldn't do it.'

'I'm struggling with this as well, but … '

'We don't have any real, direct evidence against

her. Just Catchpole's note and the word of a stupid doctor.'

'You might have by morning – if her DNA turns up at the crematorium.'

'It won't,' Lexi snapped.

'Even if she didn't put in a personal appearance, she could be the leader of the gang, directing operations from home or anywhere else. In that case, we'll have to find out some other way if she's got blood on her hands. An awful lot of it.'

'You can't believe that. She's not cruel. She's passionate about everything biological.'

Troy shrugged. 'Split personality?'

'Come off it!'

'Have you ever seen her get angry?'

'No. Well … She got annoyed with a student who came in late for one of her practicals. But that's a different league. No one got killed.'

'What was she doing in the practical?'

'Dissecting a rat.'

Troy gazed at his partner and said, 'So, she's not passionate about everything biological. Something got killed.'

'It was a rat, Troy. And it was sacrificed for a good reason – to teach us about internal organs.'

'A lab rat's not a tiger, I know, and being annoyed

isn't the same as completely blowing a fuse. I bet the rat thought she was cruel, though.'

'I'm going to call Terabyte,' Lexi said, reaching for her mobile. 'He can help with phone records and that sort of thing. He might find something definite on what she did after she left us by the side of the road last Thursday.'

Troy nodded. 'It'd be good to know if she's got an alibi – or if she talked to somebody near the crematorium.'

SCENE 26

Thursday 22nd May, Afternoon

Troy thought that, working closely with Lexi, he'd got used to outer food, but his stomach turned at the sight of Terabyte tucking into mopane worms with onions. Despite their name, mopane worms were large black and yellow caterpillars. Once cooked, they looked disgusting. They shrivelled into a dark brown tube, with the head still clearly visible as a black blob at one end. And they sounded disgusting. While he worked, Terabyte scrunched them between his teeth.

Lexi watched her partner's pained expression and

chuckled. 'Do you want to try some? Savoury, salty and crunchy.'

Joining in, Terabyte added, 'A good source of iron, calcium and phosphorus.'

Lexi said, 'They're farmed, not endangered.'

'You'd have to cover them completely in chocolate,' Troy replied. 'Even then ... They're north of revolting. Fried crickets look shiveringly good in comparison.'

'Right,' Terabyte said, spinning round on his chair. 'News and no news. The number you know for Florrie Tamsin Two's phone wasn't used at all last Thursday night. She took a call from you, Lexi, in the afternoon. From the crash site. After that, nothing. But even an unused mobile stays connected to a network, so I can tell you she went home and that's where her phone stayed. What I can't tell you is whether she stayed at home with it or if she's got some other phone she did use that night.'

'So no proof she was involved in the crematorium action,' said Lexi.

Troy nodded. 'And no proof she contacted the gang to tell them where Joe Catchpole crashed.'

Terabyte smiled. 'Maybe you're wrong about human intervention.'

'Oh?'

'Think about technology.'

'What do you mean?' Troy asked.

'What if the van had a hidden transmitter?' Terabyte replied. 'A tracking device. Put there in secret by your bad guys to keep tabs on Joe Catchpole and his precious loads. If they thought you'd find it on a complete strip-down, they'd be keen to get the van back – in case you traced them through it.'

'Nice thinking. North of nice,' Troy said. 'And if you're right, it changes everything. They'd know where the van was all the time.'

Lexi agreed. 'No need for Florrie – or anybody else – to leak the information.'

'They'd know where to look for Catchpole, grab him off the streets and finish him off in the furnace as punishment. If he did end up in the crematorium.'

Clearly, Lexi felt relief but, out of habit, she muttered, 'We'll see.'

Terabyte swivelled to face his computer again. 'I'm still thinking about Florrie Tamsin Two.' He chomped some more mopane worms.

'What are you thinking?' said Lexi.

'I'll tell you when I've thought it.'

Troy warned his partner, 'She's not off the hook, Florrie Two. We've got a witness who swears she's the gang leader. And Joe Catchpole wrote her name and address down.'

Interrupting, Terabyte said, 'That's what I'm thinking about.'

'Is this thinking going to take a long time?' Lexi asked.

'Maybe. Maybe not. I'll let you know.'

'I'm taking a meditation break,' Lexi said, 'then I'm off to the lab. I'm going to speed the crematorium samples through as quick as I can.'

SCENE 27

Troy was about to tell Lexi what was troubling him, but she got in before him. 'First full result. The denim fibres at the crematorium are chemically identical to the van driver's. The jeans are a fairly common type, but it's still looking grim for Catchpole.'

'No DNA to back it up yet?'

'I've fast-tracked the samples but it'll be tomorrow morning.'

'Okay.'

'Have you come to tell me something?'

'Our chat with Henry Patrick Fifteen,' Troy

replied. 'I replayed it on my life-logger, just to be sure. Some things don't add up. I don't trust him, but I think I know what's going on.'

'Oh?'

'It's strange that he spilled the beans before I got the chief to promise him a new ID overseas. If it was all for real and as dangerous for him as he claimed, he would've kept quiet till a deal was signed, sealed and delivered. That could mean he wasn't telling us the truth about the animal traffickers. He didn't have to worry about getting a new ID because he wasn't shopping the bad guys.'

'Go on.'

'I think it was genuine when he let that 'she' slip. Then, when I mentioned Florrie Tamsin Two, he saw an opportunity to steer us away from the 'she' and towards someone he'd never heard of. When he got going, he was vague. North of vague. No names, places, dates, times. He *had* to be because he knows absolutely nothing about Florrie.'

'Makes sense.'

'In the first half,' Troy said, 'it was too dangerous to talk. He wouldn't be safe anywhere. Second half, he changed his tune. Suddenly he's okay with the idea of a new ID and a one-way plane ticket. That's because he decided to dump Florrie in it, not the real bad guy.'

Terabyte came into the laboratory like a missile through the wall. 'Thinking completed successfully,' he announced.

'Let's hear it,' said Lexi.

'All right. Remember Joe Catchpole wrote Florrie Tasmin Two instead of Tamsin? Easy mistake to make. But I was wondering if there was more to it. Was it a spelling mistake or did he copy her name down accurately from somewhere that got it wrong? For the last few hours, it looked like a simple mistake because I couldn't find any site that called her Tasmin.'

'But?' Troy prompted.

'I dug deeper into the web. That's why it's taken a while. To cut a long story short, the first version of her latest article on endangered species had a typo. Somehow her name came out as Florrie *Tasmin* Two. It was corrected after a few days online and the original was removed. But I found it, buried deep in the web's backwater. I've got a copy of the deleted file, quoting the author as Florrie Tasmin Two.'

'So, you think Catchpole was surfing about animal extinction and he saw it before it was altered,' said Troy. 'That's where he got the Tasmin from.'

Terabyte nodded. 'Yes. What he put down for her work address was exactly how it appeared in the article as well.'

Lexi and Troy exchanged a glance. 'Maybe he wanted to consult an expert about the animals he was carrying,' Troy suggested. 'Nothing sinister. Just his natural curiosity coming out to play.'

Shrugging, Terabyte replied, 'It's a theory.'

Troy smiled. 'Time to talk to Henry Patrick Fifteen again.'

'You first met Joe Catchpole in prison, didn't you?' Troy asked.

'Yes,' the doctor answered.

'Tell me about him.'

'Tell you what about him?' Henry Fifteen replied.

'You treated his food poisoning and talked to him about being a courier.'

'Yes.'

'He agreed to become the gang's driver?'

'When he was released, yes.'

'Why not just use a modern van and program it?'

Henry shrugged. 'I wouldn't know, but I assume Florrie Two wanted deliveries to be more flexible. You could ask her. If you dare.'

'Perhaps she liked a human in control so she knew who to blame – and punish – for any mistakes.'

Henry's smile was twisted. 'You may have a point.'

Troy was not yet ready to move on to Florrie Two. 'You described Joe Catchpole as talkative.'

'Too talkative. He asked too many questions.'

'Such as?'

'Who, what, where, why.'

'Did he ever express an interest in the animals themselves?'

'Yes.'

'I suspect you didn't tell him much,' Troy said. 'Maybe he looked something up. A bit of online research.'

'Now you mention it, he told me he'd read an article about animals on the verge of extinction.'

Troy remained calm. He sighed as if he was not really getting the information he wanted. 'And what was he going to do about it? Resign out of pity?'

'No.'

'What then?'

'He said he was going to contact the author to find out more. I warned him against it, but it probably had no effect. He was inquisitive.'

'Who wrote this article?'

'A biologist,' Henry said. 'A conservationist, I imagine.'

'Did he tell you a name?'

'No.'

'I want to take you back to this morning,' Troy said. 'You told me that Florrie Tamsin Two runs the trade in endangered animals. Yes?'

'Yes.'

'And you said you know this because Joe Catchpole told you. He mentioned her name, you said.'

'Yes.'

'But Catchpole didn't mention the name of the author.'

'No.'

Troy sat back in his chair. 'Well, that's weird.'

'In what way?'

'I would have thought, when he told you about the article, he'd tell you that it was written by the same woman who pays both of you to trade endangered species. Florrie Tamsin Two.'

Henry Patrick Fifteen wilted visibly in his seat.

'Don't you find that surprising?' Troy asked.

'No comment.'

'Could it be that you just made it up? Joe Catchpole never mentioned Florrie Two at all, did he?'

'No comment.'

'You're definitely looking at a charge of perverting the course of justice now. Unless you admit it was a silly mistake and make up for it by telling us who the real leader is.'

'No comment.'

SCENE 28

Friday 23rd May, Early morning

Troy had still not fully caught up on sleep but he rose early, eager to hear about Lexi's overnight results. First, he grabbed some breakfast. If Lexi had been in the kitchen with him, he had no doubt that she would have told him gleefully that his cereal contained lots of hidden insect fragments. Afterwards, he wolfed down a fry-up and then charged out of the door into the waiting car.

He joined his partner in the forensic lab. At once, he could tell from her expression that she had made significant progress. She looked pleased, tired and satisfied. Behind all that, there was also some anxiety.

'Who won?' he prompted. 'The flames, or forensic science?'

'Huh. No contest,' she replied. 'I got a perfect match with Joe Catchpole's DNA. When someone bundled his body into the oven, a hair and some skin scraped against the outside and fell onto the floor. There, the heat wasn't enough to destroy the molecules. There was a drop of his blood on the floor as well.'

Troy nodded. 'Add murder of humans to the murder of endangered animals.'

'I found – and eliminated – two more DNA profiles. They belong to the staff.'

'For now, let's assume they weren't involved.'

'There was more DNA on the rake and inside the gloves. Two other male majors. They've both got police records for a whole series of crimes: theft, mugging and that sort of thing.'

'There's something you're not telling me.'

Lexi took a deep breath. 'I found one other DNA profile on the tongs,' she said hesitantly. 'It's ... interesting. Not Florrie Tamsin Two,' she stressed. 'A female major. It's not in our database but there's a partial match.'

'Yes?'

'You're not going to like it.'

Troy shrugged. 'Whether I like it or not doesn't affect the result. Get it over with.'

'It's a close match with Eddie Nolan, the gangster your mother ... '

Troy interrupted. 'I know who Eddie Nolan is. And I know what my mum did.'

Before Troy was old enough to know anything about crime, his mother was a police officer. Off-duty, she saw two lads with guns about to shoot a much older man. She didn't know at the time that the older man was Eddie Nolan, the godfather of a notorious gang. Thinking it was a mugging, she protected him with her body. She died from the bullets that were meant for Eddie Nolan. To show his gratitude, Eddie rewarded Troy's dad, also a police officer. Winston Goodhart got all sorts of favours. And he was paid to turn a blind eye when Eddie's gang went about their activities. The relationship between Winston Goodhart and Eddie Nolan came to an end when Troy's dad was convicted of corruption and sent to Pickling Prison. The relationship between a young Troy and his dad came to an end at the same time. Their separation became permanent exactly two weeks ago, when Winston Goodhart was caught in the Pickling Prison fire and died.

Lexi reached out and briefly grasped her partner's arm. Grateful for the small gesture, Troy closed his eyes for a moment. When he opened them, he swallowed and nodded at his partner. 'You said it was a partial match.'

'A strong partial match.'

'Does that mean it was someone in Eddie Nolan's family?'

'Yes. A very close blood relative. His mother's not alive, so a sister or daughter.'

Troy sighed. 'You must have looked his family up.'

'Yes. Eddie died two years ago. He was stabbed.'

Troy could not find any regret in his heart. He muttered, 'Live by the knife, die by the knife.'

'The one who held this particular knife confessed and is doing time right now. Name of Zak Yelland. Anyway, Nolan never had a sister. He had two sons. Both went into legitimate businesses. He also had a daughter, Pru. She was a teenage tearaway and now widely rumoured to have taken over from her father. No convictions. We haven't even got close to a prosecution. Here's the bit that'll be familiar. She has a fearsome reputation.'

'Florrie's just been replaced at the top of the list.'

'Yeah. I guess it means we pay Pru Nolan a visit. In full body armour,' she added as a joke.

Troy read Lexi's body language. She wasn't as relaxed as she pretended. Troy was even more cautious. 'If it gets around that we're on to her, she might pay *us* a visit.'

'Is that what you're suggesting?' Lexi asked. 'For you and me to be human bait?'

'No. I'm just saying that confronting her right now isn't the only option. Let's have a think first.'

'What's on your mind?'

'The Nolans and Goodharts have a history. We might be able to use that. I could offer her my services, just like Dad … '

'No chance. That'd mean going in on your own. We couldn't even wire you for sound. It'd be too dangerous. You know her reputation. You could end up as a pile of hot ashes or face-down in a lake or something equally nasty. And permanent.'

'How about we come at this from a different angle?'

Lexi sighed. 'Like?'

'Eddie Nolan's murder. I bet you checked it out.'

'Cleanest, easiest case ever,' Lexi replied. 'Zak Yelland's fingerprints and DNA on the knife and he admitted doing it. Only one thing's a bit strange.'

'What's that?'

'No known motive. He never said why he killed

his boss. He was part of the Nolan scene, so everyone assumed it was a settling of scores within the gang.' She shrugged. 'Has that got anything to do with it?'

Troy paused for a few seconds. 'Possibly.'

'What's on your mind?'

'I'm just thinking about Pru Nolan. She lost a father and gained an awful lot of power and money. Mixed emotions, maybe. Or maybe not. Why don't we find out before we tackle her?'

'How do we do that?'

'We talk to Zak Yelland.'

SCENE 29

Friday 23rd May, Late morning

Troy had been suspicious about Zak Yelland and his motives even before arriving at the prison and passing through the three locked and guarded gates. Once inside, Troy was soon sure that there was a story yet to be revealed.

Yelland had been given the best jobs in the high-security prison. There had to be a reason why he'd gained such privileges, but no one was sure. Or maybe no one wanted to admit the reason. The staff muttered something about good behaviour, but Troy knew there must be something more. Zak also had the respect of the guards and other prisoners. Compared to most of the inmates, he was pampered.

He was wearing the usual orange prison uniform. Middle-aged and stocky, he had a neck so short that his head seemed to sit directly on his body and his chin almost touched his chest. He was probably powerful but cumbersome in movement. The fingers of his right hand were crooked and scarred.

Two guards stood to attention outside the sparse room as Troy went straight for the heart of the matter. 'Why did you kill Eddie Nolan?'

'We ... er ... didn't see eye to eye on all things.'

Troy jerked a thumb towards his partner, sitting next to him. 'I don't suppose Detective Lexi Four agrees with everything I say and do, but she hasn't knifed me.'

'My solicitor told me never to talk about it.'

'Really?' Troy didn't believe it, so he tried a bluff. 'My commander told me never to talk about confidential information I get from solicitors but ... ' He shrugged. 'I don't think it's your solicitor who's stopping you.'

'Let me put it this way. My family's important to me. No one disrespects them.'

'What did Nolan do that annoyed you so much?'

Zak shook his head and folded his arms tightly across his chest.

His refusal to speak did not surprise Troy. Increasingly, he got the impression that Zak was hiding the truth. Troy tried a new tactic. 'Okay. Here's something else that was never explained. You attacked Nolan with a knife. A large knife. He had multiple wounds about the neck and arms, according to the pathology report. I understand that. But what about the small cut here?' Troy bent down and touched his left leg. 'Why did you stab him behind the knee?'

'It's all a bit of a blur to tell you the truth. I did kill him, though. I think I was … Yes. I was walking away. He was on the ground. Face down. I slipped. Dropped the knife. It landed on the back of his knee.'

'Are you sure about that?'

'Yes. Now you mention it, I'm certain.'

Troy nodded. 'Well, that's way north of weird.'

'Why?'

'Because I just made it up.'

'What?'

'There were no wounds on his legs.'

'So, why did you … ?'

Troy said, 'Because I think the whole thing's a lie – and I wondered if you'd go along with a made-up injury in some daft attempt to make sure you look guilty.'

'But ... '

'You're taking the rap for someone else, aren't you?'

'No.'

'You didn't kill him. You just put your fingers round the murder weapon and confessed.'

'That's ... more than crazy,' Zak spluttered unconvincingly, his cheeks turning red.

'But it's true as well,' said Troy. 'You see, when someone's spinning me a lie, I see through it. Especially if it's a bad-luck story like yours. If you know you're not very convincing, you look embarrassed. If your act is going well and you think you'll get away with it, a bit of delight – some pride – creeps into the performance. That's out of sync with a sob story. Either way, it's easy to spot. Right now, you're ashamed, wishing you were a better actor.'

'What are you talking about?'

'Someone's got such a hold on you, you'll stay in here for years. You're the sacrificial lamb for someone else's crime. How come they've got such power over you? How did they persuade you to take the rap?'

'I don't know what you mean.'

'Someone's pulling the strings behind the scenes. That's why you've got respect and privileges.'

'No!'

'You mentioned family. They're important to you. Are they getting some sort of reward for you being in here? Don't lie because we'll check. If they've been living really well since the murder – plenty of cash – it'll be obvious.'

'I'm guilty. I killed him!' Zak was so frustrated and frightened, he nearly shouted.

'You're scared by the idea of innocence, aren't you? You don't want to be released. Would she class that as a mistake? Would she punish you? Is that the problem?'

Zak shook his head firmly.

Troy noted that he wasn't at all surprised when he referred to 'she'. He pushed his luck a little further. 'Or would she punish your relatives? Is that the power she's got over you? Your family's okay as long as you keep on pretending to be guilty and stay inside?'

This time, Zak's head drooped completely onto his chest. Several seconds passed before he whispered, 'No.'

'What happened to your hand?'

Zak stroked his misshapen fist with his left hand.

'I thumped too many people with rock-solid chins.'
He tried to smile.

'It wasn't someone torturing you, then? Breaking
each finger till you agreed to do something.'

'No.'

'Is the Nolan gang involved in smuggling
endangered animals into the country?'

Scratching his cheek with his damaged fingers,
Zak hesitated before attempting to lie. 'What for? I
haven't come across it.'

'How did Pru Nolan get on with her father?' Troy
asked. 'Was she eager for him to stand aside and hand
the reins of the business over to her?'

'I wouldn't know.'

Troy let out a long breath. 'Well, I don't think
you're guilty. I think someone else had a motive
for getting rid of him. Not you. I'm sure there's
been a miscarriage of justice, so I'm going to do
you a favour and start a campaign to get you out
of here.'

'No. You can't do that!'

'Why not?'

'Because ... '

'Because what?'

'You just can't.'

'We can protect your family. You tell me their

names and I'll have them out of the country with new identities. You join them when you're released.'

Zak shook his head. 'I won't be released.'

Troy could see moisture in Zak's eyes. He saw immense sorrow. And he understood. 'You mean she's got people in here who are watching your every move.'

For an instant, Zak glanced towards the officers on duty outside the interview room.

Feeling a deep compassion for this trapped and tortured man, Troy nodded. 'Guards and other prisoners. If they got a whiff of a deal ... '

Zak wiped his face but said nothing.

Troy stood up. 'All right. No campaign. But we'll do our best to bring Pru and her gang to its knees. Then, maybe ... '

Walking back towards the car, Lexi chuckled. 'You've just set a new standard. I've seen detectives failing to get crooks to admit they're guilty, but I've never seen anyone failing to get a prisoner to admit he's innocent.'

Troy sighed. 'He's scared stiff – for himself and even more for his family.'

'You're the perceptive one, but even I spotted that.'

'We've got to end it,' said Troy. 'We've got to wipe her out, Lexi.'

'I know.'

SCENE 30

Friday 23rd May, Afternoon

'Pru Nolan.' The commander groaned and shook his head. 'She's untouchable. She's got friends in all sorts of unexpected places.'

Standing in front of the chief's wide desk, Troy put his head on one side. 'Friends?'

'All right. Point taken. People under her control.'

'Friends stick with you through thick and thin,' Troy replied. 'These people aren't her friends. They're paid or petrified. Every kid learns this in school: extract a bully's teeth and their support crumbles. Take Pru Nolan out and we'll have a queue of people desperate to testify against her. Then we'll be able to wrap this case – and probably plenty of others – up.'

'But, right now, you've only got evidence she was at the crematorium where Joe Catchpole appears to have gone up in flames.'

'Her and two of her heavies,' said Lexi.

'It's enough to get the ball rolling,' Troy claimed. 'We need a warrant to get into Henry Patrick Fifteen's bank account. We want to see what happens to the money he earns from selling natural medicines. If he transfers most of it to Pru Nolan, we've got her.'

The commander nodded. 'Fair enough. I'll get Terabyte to move on that. As for tackling Nolan herself … ' He sighed and shook his head. 'You don't have enough evidence to nail her. Her lawyer's going to argue she was in the crematorium a day or two after – or a day or two before – Joe Catchpole. You can't prove they were there at the same time. And you don't have a body. Or a weapon.'

'The weapon's the furnace,' Lexi replied. 'We've got Nolan's DNA in the same room but, no, it's not the same as her fingerprints on the gun that fired the fatal bullet.'

'I suppose you could question her as a potential witness,' the chief said.

'We really need your go-ahead,' Troy prompted.

'Are you sure that's what you want to do?'

'Yes,' they said in unison.

'It's not an enviable assignment. I can't think of a more dangerous one.'

Neither of them wavered.

He stared at them for five long seconds. 'All right. Look after each other. Okay?'

'Okay.'

'Particularly you, Lexi. There's history between the Goodharts and the Nolan family – as you know – so watch over your partner.'

'Like a hawk,' she replied.

SCENE 31

Friday 23rd May, Late afternoon

To Troy and Lexi, Pru Nolan's mansion was a lion's den. Even so, they walked into it willingly. Standing in the flashy reception room, Troy wondered whether his father had waited to receive payment or instructions from Pru's father in exactly the same spot. If he had, Troy also wondered if his father's heart had thumped as much as his was doing right now.

On the walls were gaudy modern – and probably expensive – paintings. On the furniture were showy vases and glasswork. Two upright male figures were probably made of solid gold. A large, loud pendulum swinging underneath an ornamental clock signalled the passing of time. The décor belonged to someone with more money than taste.

In the corner of the room, a parrot sat on a perch. Bright green, red and blue, the bird was as flamboyant as its surroundings. It leaned forward to get a good look at the two visitors and then shrieked, 'Scum!'

Troy turned to Lexi and smiled weakly. 'Can't think who it learned that from.'

When Pru Nolan walked into the room, the parrot seemed to straighten up and it cried, 'Pretty woman.'

Pru was in her mid-thirties. She was precisely made up with vivid red lipstick. Her hair was straight and neat, cut severely at the shoulder. It was too black to be a natural colour. Despite her age, she oozed glamour. She probably controlled her appearance as much as she controlled the people in her gang. Behind her were two muscular minders.

Troy pointed to his life-logger and said, 'We're recording this.'

'You haven't heard that I don't speak to the police.'

'We're different.'

Pru laughed. 'In what way?'

Troy waved towards his partner and said, 'This is

Detective Lexi Iona Four and I'm Detective Troy Goodhart.' He stressed his surname.

Pru stared at him for a moment and then smirked. 'Goodhart. That's a name to conjure with.'

'So, you know about it. How my mum saved your dad's life.'

'And how my dad paid his debt to yours.'

'Yes.'

'We're already quits. But you're right. It makes you different. I will try to be patient with a Goodhart.' She fixed her gaze on Lexi and said, 'But an outer police officer … ' It was a deadly serious comment – and a threat – but it ended with a sly smile, as if she were teasing.

The parrot screeched, 'Scum.'

Pru's expression softened and she focused again on Troy. 'My father died. He was stabbed. Yours?'

'Mine died as well. Two weeks ago. But he died a hero, saving people from a fire.'

'Hero or villain. Makes no difference. When they're gone, they're gone. Anyway, these labels are deceptive, aren't they?' Pru said mischievously. 'Who decides who's the hero and who's the villain? My dad wasn't in prison. Yours was, wasn't he?'

'Yes.'

'There. See what I mean? Life's complicated.'

'Is it? Either something's against the law or it isn't. Simple. The rest is down to who gets caught and who doesn't.'

Pru laughed. 'Like father, like son – or daughter. You became a detective and I took over my father's business.'

Troy nodded. Provoking her, he said, 'You need to prove you're tougher than him.'

'And why are you here? Not to ask for favours. That's all in the past.' She made herself comfortable in a chair but did not invite the detectives to sit down. 'If you wanted an arrangement like the one between our fathers, you'd have come on your own. You're here to prove you're a better police officer than your dad.'

'Pretty woman,' the parrot announced.

'Who murdered your father?'

'A man called Zak Yelland. Some sort of family dispute.'

'No,' Troy said. 'I mean, who *really* killed him?'

Pru creased up her face and shook her head. 'Are you completely insane?'

'Where were you and what were you doing last Thursday night?' he asked.

'I was right here, doing nothing. Chilling. How many people do you want to confirm that?'

Troy smiled, even though his mouth was dry and his heart rate had rocketed. 'It doesn't count if they do it out of loyalty or because they're scared of you. What were you doing with Catchpole in the crematorium?'

Pru lifted up her bare arms, pretending to be puzzled again. 'I wasn't.'

Calling up his reserves of bravado, Troy replied, 'That's not what Joe says.'

Pru's mouth opened in surprise but she stopped herself from saying anything.

Troy cursed inwardly. He had hoped that she would fall into his trap and tell him that Catchpole was dead. If she had, he would have asked how she knew.

'Okay,' she said a moment later, once she'd recovered. 'Wheel him in. Let's hear what's on his mind.'

'Have you been in the crematorium?'

'Yes.'

'When?'

'When my father died.'

'And did you go in the cremation chamber itself?'

'No.'

'Since then?'

'No.'

'But we can prove you have. Along with two of your thugs. How do you explain that?'

Looking at Lexi, Pru replied, 'Easy. You got your forensics wrong.'

Lexi shook her head. 'No chance.'

'It happens all the time. Put an expensive toy in the hands of someone young and incompetent … ' She shrugged. 'Mistaken identity. I could lend you a couple of my people, if you like. They'll soon sort it out. Give you a second opinion and show you where you're going wrong.'

'Thanks for the offer,' Troy replied, 'but our tests were good and so's Lexi.'

Pru stood up again. 'I said I'd be as patient as possible, but I've reached my limit. Look. You could carry on with your investigation and live with the consequences or apologise and drop it. Since you're a Goodhart, I'll forget you ever came here and questioned my integrity. No hard feelings. It's a good deal.'

'We only close a case when it's done and dusted – and someone's charged,' said Troy.

'Our fathers would have come to an agreement, no doubt. It's a shame we can't do the same.' She paused significantly and said, 'Goodbye.'

Her pet parrot squawked, 'Scum!'

Walking back to the car, Lexi said, 'Maybe the plan wasn't to become human bait but … '

Troy nodded. 'We've succeeded anyway.'

'Yeah. What's her next move going to be, perceptive partner?'

'She could try and buy us off or ruin us. You know. Giant sums of money in our bank accounts or bags or whatever. Either we accept the money – bought off – or a high-up discovers it and we're discredited. But I think that's how the older generation did it. The Eddie Nolan way. This generation – Pru – gives it more welly. Brute force.' Troy opened the car door but hesitated before getting in. 'I think she'll want to steamroller us so no one else will dare to take up the case afterwards.'

'We need to be ready for rough stuff.'

'Very.'

SCENE 32

Saturday 24th May, The early hours

In the dead of night, a shrill repetitive sound spoiled the stillness and roused Troy from a deep sleep. His mind fogged, he answered the phone. 'Troy Goodhart,' he mumbled.

A distraught voice brought him to his senses immediately. 'She's been taken, Troy,' Terabyte almost shouted.

'You mean Lexi?'

'Yes.'

'Taken?'

'Snatched off the street. I'm sending you the video

from her life-logger. The last bit before it was destroyed.'

'I'm getting up.'

The camera in Lexi's life-logger had switched automatically to night-vision mode. The video showed four indistinct gangsters in balaclavas. The scene reminded Troy of the hijack of the pick-up truck and the crashed van. According to the witnesses, that snatch had been executed perfectly by five people wearing balaclavas. The taking of Lexi Iona Four was much more difficult. She kicked and punched two of her attackers to the floor. But eventually she was outnumbered and overwhelmed. She took a blow to the back of the head with a baseball bat and her resistance was over. The same man then battered her life-logger with the heavy club. Job done.

The kitchen door opened and, bleary-eyed, Gran entered.

'Oh. Sorry. I tried not to disturb you,' said Troy.

'Since your dad … I don't sleep much. Something's bothering you. What is it, honey?'

He took a deep breath. 'Lexi's been snatched.'

'You mean, someone's grabbed her?'

'Yes.'

Gran looked at her grandson sympathetically. 'You like her, don't you? Despite … '

'Yes, Gran. I do.'

'You've got to do something about it, then. Not stand here chatting to me.'

'I'm on my way.'

'Who's taken her? Do you know?'

'The Eddie Nolan gang.'

For a second, Gran hesitated. Then, angry, she growled, 'The man who ruined your father.'

'It's his daughter, Pru.'

'I know that girl.'

'Really?'

'Well, your dad talked about her a few times. She was trouble, he said. A right handful. She's got the same rotten genes as her no-good father.'

'Worse,' Troy replied.

Gran nodded. 'You go and sort that family out for good. It's about time someone did. I'd do it myself if … '

'I'm off, Gran.'

'Be careful, honey.'

There were two cars waiting in the street. One was a police car. The other had two of Pru's minders inside. Troy paused for a moment and then went to the second car.

One of the henchmen lowered the window.

'You sent four to get Lexi. Only two for me. You think I won't put up a fight because you've got my partner.'

The man bared ugly teeth.

'Let's not mess about,' Troy said. 'If I go off, you'll follow and tackle me later. A waste of your time and mine.'

'Leave your camera and mobile here.'

Troy went to the police car and threw his life-logger and phone onto one of the seats.

When he returned, the gangster opened the door and said, 'Get in.'

The car pulled away and Troy accepted a blindfold over his eyes.

In his house, the curtain fell back into place as his grandmother withdrew from the window.

SCENE 33

Saturday 24th May, Before dawn

When the blindfold was removed, Troy's arms and ankles were tied securely to a chair in some sort of lounge. There were pictures of yachts on two of the walls.

Pru was sipping a juice and smiling triumphantly. Beside her, there was a laptop and a large screen. And a handgun.

'Where am I?' said Troy.

Pru did not dodge the question. 'It's a private marina. I bet your dad would have known it. My father did a lot of business here. This is the clubhouse.' She nodded towards the blank screen. 'This is for watching films.'

Troy shuddered. He realized immediately that he was in danger because she answered his question. She would have been far more evasive, he thought, if she expected him to walk away from this encounter. Plainly, she was confident that she was in control and that, one way or another, he would have no use for information. He'd been blindfolded to disorient and dishearten him, rather than to conceal his whereabouts.

'Out there,' she said, waving towards the window at the back of the room, 'there's a lake and boats. That's where the action is.'

'You mean Lexi?'

Pru grinned. 'Detective Lexi Iona Four. Yes.'

'What are you doing to her?'

'I have three fantastic yachts. Expensive boats. I have a couple I'm not proud of, but I keep them because they serve a purpose. You know what I mean? They work. Then there's an old wreck. Actually, that has a purpose as well. A last purpose. You see, it's leaking. It won't still be afloat by the time the sun comes up.'

Troy guessed what was coming. 'That's where you've put Lexi.'

Using the laptop, Pru put a live video feed on the screen. It wasn't a film. It showed Lexi. She was standing alone next to a handrail in the small, dismal cabin of a boat. Both of her wrists were shackled and the chain binding them passed behind the rail. She was trapped.

Leaning against the cabin wall, she looked dazed, but Troy knew she wasn't hurt. He'd seen that expression before. She was conserving energy, trying to bring down her metabolic rate through complete relaxation. Troy imagined that she'd already yanked on the chains and the handrail. She must have decided that both were unbreakable.

'I've left the battery running,' said Pru. 'I don't know how long it'll hold out, but it provides power for the boat's lights. Look at her feet. She's paddling already.'

'What do you want?'

Pru laughed. 'I don't need to tell you that. No one likes the police poking around.'

'So, we drop the case. What do we get in return?'

'Look carefully at the chain. See? There's a combination lock. There's a small monitor next to the camera. You can't see it, but she can. I can display the code that'll unlock the catch. Your colleague can then release herself and swim for it. I hope she can swim. I didn't check.'

'How do I know you're not making it up?'

'She's good-looking in a strange, outer sort of way, isn't she? Watch her. I'll give her the wrong combination.'

Pru punched a four-digit number on the keyboard and transmitted it.

Lexi became alert and her eyes told Troy that she was reading from a panel just to the right of the camera. Then she twisted her fingers, fiddling with the chain till she had the lock in her right hand. She aligned the four numbers with her left hand and pulled maddeningly on the catch. Nothing moved. Frustrated, she gave up.

Troy tried to read her face. Had she realized that she'd been put through a dummy run? He wasn't sure. She let out a breath and her shoulders drooped again.

'Tell me what I want to hear – call off the enquiry and promise it won't be taken up by anybody else – and you'll see me give her the right code. You'll see her escape.'

Troy shook his head.

'Plenty of time to change your mind,' she said. 'The water's barely at her knees.' Pru sipped her drink and continued, 'Actually, I was thinking of reversing the roles. You out there and your mate

197

in here. But no. She might've been prepared to watch you die – for the sake of a pointless investigation. Outers are like that. But you … You're more emotionally attached. You're a major. You think human life is more important than detective work.'

'That's not the point,' Troy replied, looking defiantly at his captor.

'Enlighten me.'

'I could agree to all sorts in exchange for her life – and mine, maybe – but I'm not sure you'd keep your side of the bargain. Your track record is south of good.'

Troy believed that Pru Nolan enjoyed punishing people. Merely dropping a case probably wasn't enough to satisfy her when she had the opportunity to make an example of two detectives. She could enhance her ruthless reputation by killing them both. She was like a cat, playing with them until she tired of the entertainment and showed her claws.

'You have my word. I'll give her the right combination and she'll swim away. Your own eyes can't lie.'

'No.'

Pru let out a little laugh. 'You're as obstinate as me. We're both more obstinate than our fathers.'

'We're not that similar, you and me. For one thing, I didn't kill my own father.'

'Neither did I. Someone else pleaded guilty to that.'

'You couldn't wait. You got rid of him and forced one of your people to take the blame. That's how come you're running the show now.'

'I said I'd be patient because you're a Goodhart, because of your mother. Ask yourself this. Does that make sense if I murdered my own father? It's more likely I'd bear your mum a grudge for saving him – and forcing me to do it instead. But that's not how it is. I'm grateful.'

'Back then, you weren't ready to take over. A couple of years ago, you were. That's my guess.'

'I'll give you one thing. He died at the right time – before his power and abilities deserted him. That's good. Life – and death – have a way of working out for the best.'

'That's convenient for you.'

Troy kept his eyes on the screen. The water was lapping around Lexi's waist. He was sure it was rising faster now.

Definitely feeling a buzz, Pru teased him further. 'You've got to hope the boat doesn't keel over. If it does, she's a goner.'

'You're enjoying this, aren't you? Better than any film.'

'I'm wondering how far up you'll let the water get before you can't stand watching it any more.'

Troy wasn't sorry he'd walked into this predicament. Sooner or later, Pru's heavies would have grabbed him anyway. And from the inside, there was always a chance that he'd spot an opportunity to salvage the situation. It had to be soon, for Lexi's sake. Even strapped to a chair, Troy could still deploy his greatest weapons: words. But he felt increasingly helpless because, so far, every one of them had bounced off Pru Nolan without leaving an impression. And the water was rising up his partner's body like an unstoppable incoming tide.

SCENE 34

Saturday 24th May, Before dawn

Lexi's wrists still hurt from the hammering she'd given to the handrail. But it hadn't budged. Not even a hint of movement. And the chain between her wrists had stayed firm.

She changed tactics. Even though she was standing and cold water was creeping slowly up her legs, she tried to reduce her heart rate by deep meditation.

In life-threatening situations, outers seemed to have the ability to put their bodies into slow motion. To survive critical injuries or illnesses, super-relaxation – or mini-hibernation – gave their bodies more time to repair.

Lexi wasn't injured, but she was in a life-threatening situation. Soon, if she had to hold her breath and swim underwater, she would benefit if her heart rate and metabolism were so low that her body needed less air.

She had worked out what was happening, of course. It didn't take a genius. High on the opposite wall, just below the ceiling, there was a spy camera and an LED display. In the ceiling, two lamps lit up the space. By now, the Nolan gang would have captured Troy, and Pru would be torturing him with the images of her imminent drowning. Because he was a major, he would offer token resistance, but it was only a matter of time before he gave in and agreed to her demands. Presumably to halt the case. Lexi didn't know when he would concede but she guessed that the water would get much higher yet. Then the small monitor would show her the combination to the lock that held the chains in place.

There had already been a false display. That was probably for Troy's benefit – to prove to him that she could read the code.

But would Nolan ever reveal the right combination? Even if she did, was the room locked?

Perhaps Lexi would be able to break free of the chain but not escape the cabin. If the spy camera still worked when it was fully submerged, Troy would then witness her frantic and doomed attempts to swim to safety. But if the idea was to convince Troy that she could get away unharmed, Nolan might have planned something worse beyond the cabin and out of camera shot.

Actually, Lexi would prefer to die serenely in the water, still bound but relaxed beyond pain, than be freed by Troy's promises and killed later by a bunch of paid thugs.

The water continued to rise up her body. Really, it was the other way round. Along with the wreck, she was slowly sinking into the water. She didn't mind the chill that was engulfing her centimetre by centimetre. She welcomed its cooling effect on her metabolism. It helped her remain calm. It also provided uplift. The incoming lake supported more and more of her weight, allowing her to save more energy. Soon, she would be able to float, like the feeling of a peaceful meditation. But she wouldn't close her eyes for long. She needed to see that small monitor next to the camera.

She knew she was being watched, so she didn't feel alone and abandoned. But she did feel like an exhibit. More than an exhibit. Recalling Florrie's laboratory and its tanks of pond life, she imagined her behaviour in this cabin was also being studied and assessed.

Using her feet, she prised off both shoes and then she wriggled out of her trousers. They were sodden and threatened to weigh her down. The shackles stopped her removing her top. She lay back and floated, staring at the roof above her head. All the time, she was getting closer to the rusting metal and the lights. She wondered whether she would run out of air and suffocate before she drowned. It didn't matter. The consequence was the same.

Nurturing inner stillness, she drifted on the lake and left her fate in the hands of her partner.

SCENE 35

Saturday 24th May, Before dawn

Watching her victim remove her shoes and trousers, Pru said, 'Looks to me like she's getting ready for a swim. That means she expects you to fold. She wants you to fold. She's sending you a message.'

'Not true. There's no message. She's trying to unwind.' But Troy knew that what helped her to relax also made her more able to swim.

By switching to a horizontal position, Lexi had stopped Troy gauging the water level simply by watching it creep up her chest. Now he had to estimate the distance between her upturned face and the ceiling. He was also aware that the volume of air available for her to breath was decreasing all the time.

'Remember, you've got to give her time to undo the lock,' Pru told him. 'She might panic a bit and get it wrong. It's a fiddly job.'

'You trade endangered animals, don't you?'

She laughed aloud. 'You want me to confess now? What's the point? You're not wearing a life-logger.'

'Do you?'

'You know I do. It's very easy to separate fools from vast sums of money. You can't prove it, though.'

Troy watched Lexi floating nearer and nearer to the ceiling. He hoped she wasn't meditating, because she did that with her eyes closed. 'Lexi said something about people like you. She looked at the blood and bone in the van and said you had no humanity.' He nodded towards the screen. 'It's true.'

'You might quibble with some of my methods, but I'm effective.'

'That figures.'

Something was changing. Lexi was no longer floating peacefully. As the boat sank further, she began to struggle and kick out. Troy soon realized that the chain that joined her wrists via the handrail was not long enough to allow her to float any more. It was dragging down her hands, arms and, soon, her face.

'All right,' he cried. 'Enough! Give her the code. I'm dropping the case.'

'Completely?'

'Yes.'

'Before you leave here, you'll call your chief and tell him there's no evidence and never will be? You'll make sure no one else re-opens the investigation?'

'Yes. Let her go!'

Pru took her time. Revelling in her superiority, she tapped three digits on her laptop and then looked across at Troy. 'Maybe you wouldn't fall for rhino horn and the rest of it, but you're a fool as well. I believe you'll keep your word – if you stay alive long enough.' She tapped the final number and transmitted the code.

SCENE 36

Saturday 24th May, Before dawn

Lexi realized that the remaining space was not the main problem. It was the length of the chain. She couldn't float on her back any more. She had to turn over. Face down. She had to get her hands and arms lower in the water. She felt like a hooked fish at the surface of the lake. The tether was trying to reel her in – but downwards, towards the submerged rail. She tried not to panic, not to undo the benefit of her internal composure.

Her watery eyes caught sight of the monitor and it told her that Troy had cracked. The code was revealed in glowing green figures: 1297. But the chain wasn't long enough to bring her hands and the combination lock out of the water and up to her face. She trod water and took two deep breaths of the remaining air. After filling her lungs for the second time, she dived down with her eyes open. Fumbling with the lock, she took precious seconds to clutch it in her right hand. Her vision blurred by the soiled water, she turned the first wheel till it showed the figure 1. The second wheel slipped from her fingers twice. On the third attempt, she lined up the numbers so she had 12. The third figure was already on the number 9. Her chest felt taught and painful. The lack of oxygen was beginning to tell. Her left fingers scrambled for the final metallic wheel. Slowly, she clicked it around the ratchet. In her haste, she went straight past 7. Adjusting her grip, her lungs crying out for air, feeling like they were about to explode, she reversed the dial and aligned the numbers. 1297. The bolt fell from the contraption and the chain separated into two sections. Both were still attached to her wrists, but she was no longer bound to the handrail. She kicked her legs and executed one breaststroke with her arms.

She broke the surface and found her face was within centimetres of the ceiling. Treading water again, she gasped down as much air as she could. The top of her head was scraping against the roof of the cabin. She had only a few seconds to refill with oxygen. She realized also that she would have only one attempt to escape. By the time she'd dived down and tackled the door, the air pocket would have vanished.

She bent her neck back, keeping her face out of the water. Three times she emptied her lungs as much as possible and took great gulps of air. Then she was ready. She sealed her lips and dived back down into the lake water.

Her natural buoyancy tried to push her back up to the surface but she swam downwards with a sturdy breaststroke. It took her only seconds to locate the handle and turn it but, when she tugged, the door did not budge. She didn't believe it was locked, though. It was just the pressure of water playing tricks. She braced herself. Right hand gripping the rail, left hand around the door handle, she pulled.

She was right. It moved. It was like working in syrup, but slowly she forced the door inwards. As soon as the gap was wide enough, she swam through. And found herself in a dim, flooded corridor.

She had not been conscious when she'd been brought on board. She didn't know which way to go.

Her sight was no help at all. It was limited and indistinct. She simply swam in the direction she was pointed. Glancing to left and right, she peered through the gloom for some way to escape the wreck. Nothing. Just closed doors. She kicked hard and pulled her arms powerfully through the water, a chain dangling from each wrist. She followed the line of weakly glowing lamps in the ceiling. The pressure building in her chest and behind her eyes told her she needed an exit soon. In seconds, the impulse to open her mouth and let the exhausted air go would be irresistible.

She could see something ahead. Her sight was too fuzzy and the passageway too dark to make it out. She tried to accelerate, aware that the extra effort would deplete her oxygen level more quickly. She had little choice. But she also had determination and strength. And an immense will to escape so she could confront Pru Nolan.

When she got close, she recognized steps going upwards. Nearing exhaustion, she tipped her hands upwards and steered her body into the stairwell. A few moments later, her head broke the surface of the water, her mouth opened involuntarily and spent air erupted violently from her lungs. She gasped the cool night air. Unable at first to move, she stood, feet on one of the submerged steps and head above the rippling lake, taking breath after agonizing breath.

The marina was barely lit. Just one distant floodlight. She couldn't see a great deal, but she knew which way led to the nearest solid ground. Still panting, she took a few tired strokes to propel herself towards the moorings, like the edge of a swimming pool. It was only when she reached out with both hands and gripped the concrete that she realized that two of Nolan's heavies were standing above her in the darkness. One held a huge baseball bat in his fist. He also had his big boot firmly on the chains attached to Lexi's wrists so she could not get away. The other gangster had an axe. Its sharp blade glinted in the moonlight.

Chest still heaving, Lexi let out a groan. She was not in a position to defend herself from the blows that were about to be unleashed on her. In a twist of cruelty, Pru Nolan never intended her to survive the ordeal.

The second thug raised the heavy axe over his head. He smirked as he struck downwards.

The blade never found its mark. The axe dropped to the ground, narrowly missing Lexi's left hand as both men pitched forward into the lake.

In the place where they had been standing, Troy's grandmother appeared. She was almost shaking with fear and anger. 'Quick,' she said, bending down and offering her right hand to Lexi.

Lexi reached up, took it with both of her own hands and hauled herself out of the water. She was about to leave with Mrs Goodhart when she stopped and changed her mind. With a wicked expression on her face, she said, 'Just a second. You might want to look away.'

She was going to make sure the men were incapable of chasing them. She delivered a forward heel stomp to the first to emerge from the lake. The second got a vicious kick to his left temple and he passed out immediately.

Mrs Goodhart winced. 'It's not a good idea to make you angry, is it?'

'If it hadn't been for you, they would have killed me.'

'So it seems.'

Lexi looked into her face and nodded her thanks. 'Gran,' she panted. 'You are brilliant.'

'Us oldies have our uses.'

'In that case, do you feel like helping me rescue Troy? He got me released. Just. Time to return the favour.'

Gran stood back and looked at her from head to toe. 'Are you up to it?'

She was dripping, bare-legged and wearing the chains like grotesque bracelets. 'Oh, yes,' Lexi replied. 'I want Pru Nolan in my sights before I calm down.'

'Just tell me what to do.'

'First, we find them.'

'I think we should try over there,' said Gran. 'The big house. The lights are on and there are two cars outside. I was about to go there when I caught sight of the two men you've just clobbered.'

In her socks, Lexi felt every stone on the path but she ignored the discomfort. Striding towards the house, she realized that she had to slow down for the sake of Troy's elderly grandmother. 'How come you're here anyway?' she said softly. 'Did you follow Troy?'

'No. Winston – Troy's dad – told me about this place. He used to come here to see Eddie Nolan. I thought … maybe it's where his daughter goes about her funny business.'

'I hope you're right. Really, Troy could be anywhere. We'll see.'

Nearing the building, Lexi put her finger across her lips. She whispered, 'I'm going to sneak a look in the windows. See if he's in there. If he is, I'll need you to create a diversion. You could bang on the front door or something. Are you okay with that?'

Gran seemed worried and excited at the same time. 'I could claim I'm lost and ask for help.'

'Perfect. But stay here – by the tree – and let me check first. I'll come back and we'll sort out our timing.'

'All right, honey. Take care.'

Four minutes later, when Lexi returned to the tree, Mrs Goodhart had gone.

SCENE 37

Saturday 24th May, Dawn

Troy had just watched Lexi undo the lock and leave through the cabin door. He'd watched her swim away. But he had no real way of knowing whether she'd reached safety.

Pru interrupted his thoughts. 'Your chief's a major, I believe.'

'Yes.'

'So, he'll probably be asleep. We'll wait till he arrives at work in the morning, then you'll make a call. I'll be listening. Very carefully.'

'I want to see Lexi. I bet you've still got her.'

'That's reasonable,' Pru replied in a smarmy voice. 'After the call, she's all yours.'

The door to the lounge opened and one of Pru's minders flung a woman into the room. 'Found this one outside, snooping around.'

'Not in here!' Pru shouted at him. But then she saw the old woman and Troy Goodhart staring at each other. Troy's expression was total disbelief – and dismay. Pru put up her hand and hesitated. With a grin, she uttered, 'What have we here?' Turning again to her henchman, she said, 'It's all right. Leave us.'

Troy's first instinct was to protect his grandmother by denying all knowledge of her. He would have liked to portray her as a confused old lady who'd got lost and stumbled into the marina clubhouse by mistake. But it was already too late. Skilled in body language, he knew he'd already given the game away.

'Why don't you introduce me to your … friend?' Pru said to him.

'Er … This is a neighbour of mine. She lives just up the road. Mrs Goodall.' He turned his head towards his grandma and said, 'Mrs Goodall, this is Pru Nolan.'

'Goodall? Goodhart? Quite a coincidence.' Pru laughed unkindly. She picked up her gun. 'Now tell me the truth.'

Feeling threatened, neither of her guests responded.

Clearly amused, Pru said, 'Could it be … ?' She faked a puzzled expression. 'I see a family resemblance. Do I have the honour of entertaining another Goodhart?'

Gran took a deep breath and stared severely at Eddie Nolan's daughter. 'I'm Winston Goodhart's mother and you, my girl, need a lesson.'

Startled, Pru replied, 'And you need to remember where you are. You're on my turf now.'

'My son was a good man until … Your family's to blame.'

Pru laughed. 'I think you'll find he was an adult, responsible for his own actions.'

Still tied to the chair, Troy saw something snap within his gran. He shouted, 'No!' But it made no difference.

She'd had enough of the Nolan family. All the pain from the loss of her son spilled out of her and, arms flailing, she rushed at Pru Nolan.

Clumsily, Troy jumped to his feet. But with the chair fastened over his back, he was like a tortoise. Rigid, bent over, barely able to move.

Pru took the easy option and raised the gun.

Through the window, Lexi had seen the room where her partner was tied to a chair. There was no subtle way of making an entrance, she'd decided. She would simply follow Pru Nolan's example and use brute force. Right now, that suited her mood.

She crashed through the front door and stomped down the hallway, determined not to let anyone or anything get in her way. She met one of Nolan's thugs coming in the opposite direction. He had just come out of the room she was heading towards and he didn't stand a chance. She floored him with a flying front kick. Hardly hesitating, she stepped over him, strode to the end of the passage and turned into the room on the right. She walked in at the vital moment.

The gun in Nolan's hand fired. Troy's grandma was so close to Pru that she couldn't miss.

Gran staggered back and fell with an expression of sheer horror on her face.

Furious, Lexi didn't pause. She didn't think. Instinct took over. Chains jangling, she sprinted directly at Pru. Two bullets punctured her body, but they didn't stop her. She threw herself feet first at the gangster. In a ferocious double-footed front kick, the balls of both heels slammed into Nolan's head and chest. A chop to the neck finished her off. The ringleader was out cold before her body flopped onto the carpet.

Before attending to Mrs Goodhart and freeing Troy, Lexi staggered towards Nolan's phone. Blood running freely down her arm, she picked it up, dialled and almost yelled into it. 'Detective Lexi Iona Four. I'm at a lake and house owned by Pru Nolan. South Shepford somewhere. Trace this call. Urgent backup needed. Lots of arrests. And ambulances. One witness down. Looks in a bad way.' Almost as an afterthought, she added, 'One officer shot.'

She kicked Pru's gun away and, still in her socks and pants, knelt down beside her distraught partner. He'd managed two ungainly steps towards his grandma before crumpling helplessly to the floor. Lexi managed to undo one of his ties before she passed out.

SCENE 38

Saturday 24th May, Early afternoon

Troy sat on his own at home. The place was a void. No footsteps, no voice, no company, no one grumbling at his workload. It lacked character and colour. It lacked atmosphere. At the age of sixteen, Troy had become the senior – the only – member of his immediate family. Gran had gone.

He thought he should be doing something, but he didn't know what. He didn't have a clue. The shock had emptied him. It left him incapable. Besides, there was nothing he could do to reverse what had happened. He could not bring her back.

He imagined he felt like an outer. Alone and individual. No longer part of a clan.

There was no one else in the kitchen. He prepared a meal for one. Then, instead of eating it, he moved it aimlessly around the plate. He had a few mouthfuls and ditched the rest.

He must have left the front door open because he heard someone come in and call out his name. It was Lexi. Both detectives entered the living room from different directions at the same time.

Solemnly, Lexi said, 'I heard she didn't make it.'

'No.'

'I'm sorry, Troy.'

He didn't know what to say. He shook his head and fell into a chair.

'You don't know what she did. She saved my life. Nolan wanted you to see me escape, but I was never going to get out alive. There were two heavies waiting to finish me off. They would have done if it hadn't been for your gran. She sneaked up behind them and gave them a shove into the lake. One with each hand. She was brave and brilliant. That's why I'm still here.'

'But *she* isn't.'

'No.' Lexi sat opposite her partner. 'Do you know what I'll remember? Apart from her letting fly at those thugs.'

'No.'

'She called me honey. *Me* – an outer.'

Troy raised a slight smile.

'The last thing she said to me. "All right, honey. Take care." I'll treasure that.'

Troy looked at Lexi's left arm, supported by a sling. 'Are you okay?'

'Indestructible. One bullet removed, one went straight through. Holes plugged and bandaged up. Not serious holes. I just lost a lot of blood, so they topped me up with someone else's. It's funny. Pru Nolan tried to kill me, but she also saved me. When I run, I pump my fists in front of me. Like this.' She demonstrated as best she could with the bandages limiting her movement. 'Nolan aimed at my heart but the bullets hit the chains she'd put on me. Deflected them.'

'Good.'

'By the way,' Lexi added, 'you were right. With Pru Nolan and most of her people locked up, the chief's offered amnesties to anyone who'll testify against her. Hey presto. So far, one's said he will.'

'I wish it was Zak Yelland,' Troy replied, 'but I bet

it isn't. It'll be Henry Patrick Fifteen, squirming his way out of a prison sentence.'

Lexi smiled. 'You're good. And that's not all.'

'Oh?'

'This time we *do* have Pru Nolan's prints and DNA on the gun that fired the fatal bullet. Murder *and* attempted murder. And Terabyte tells me that Henry Fifteen's been paying money into an anonymous account that belongs to her as well. Crimes against CITES. She's going away for a long time.'

Troy nodded. He gazed at his partner and realized that, in a way, he was lucky. He had no doubt that Lexi Iona Four would be there for him when he needed a substitute family.

The real science behind the story

The crimes in all of *The Outer Reaches* books are inspired by genuine scientific issues and events. Here are a few details of the science that lies behind *Blood and Bone*.

Hunted to extinction

Some endangered animals – like the black rhino, tiger, spiny anteater, Asian bear, geckoes, turtles and saiga antelope – are being hunted to extinction to fuel the burgeoning trade for traditional Chinese 'medicine'.

An example is rhino horn for its fever-reducing properties. Tiger products are also very popular. Having them is regarded as a symbol of high status and wealth. The annual consumption of traditional remedies made of tiger bone, bear gall bladder, rhinoceros horn, dried geckoes and other animal parts is huge, making the international trade in wildlife products worth billions of pounds every year. The problem comes down to poverty. When many people live in extreme poverty and poaching one tiger can bring in ten years' worth of income on the black market, it is almost inevitable that some will be tempted into the trade. Its products are also used in the USA and UK, especially London, Birmingham, Liverpool and Manchester. In December 2013, Prince William said that the illegal trade in animal parts was 'one of the most insidious forms of corruption and criminality in the world today.'

Malcolm Rose is an established, award-winning author, noted for his gripping crime/thriller stories – all with a solid scientific basis.

Before becoming a full-time writer, Malcolm was a university lecturer and researcher in chemistry.

He says that chemistry and writing are not so different. *'In one life, I mix chemicals, stew them for a while and observe the reaction. In the other, I mix characters, stir in a bit of conflict and, again, observe the outcome.'*